THREE DAYS

TO

DIE

BY

JOHN AVERY

Second Edition, 2011
Apticon Books

ISBN: 978-0-9836963-0-8

FOR JULIE

"A temptation resisted is a true judge of character."

-- Dustin Hoffman
Papillon

Chapter 1

Snowflakes

At 9:30 a.m. that Friday, the Community Plaza Bank lobby was already crowded with customers, some scurrying about their business like hungry rodents, others unhurried, content to linger warm and dry, protected from the cold September rains blowing through the small coastal city.

None of them noticed when two small, olive-green canisters bounced softly on the carpet and rolled into the middle of the room. And when the grenades popped and began hissing out plumes of blue smoke, only an attentive few raised their eyebrows.

But when three armed thugs wearing white jumpsuits with matching Day-Glo accented ski masks burst through the doors, *everyone* noticed.

The first gunman, masked in neon-green horizontal stripes, crossed quickly to one side of the lobby and stood next to a large, marble pillar. He dropped his armload of empty duffel bags to the floor and stared back at the terrified crowd, rifle at ready.

Second through the doors, peering out through shocking-pink polka-dots, was 13-year-old Aaron Quinn. Numbed by fear, Aaron couldn't remember what to do, so he ran over and stood next to the man in neon-green.

The third gunman, in electric-blue vertical stripes under a leather fedora, moved to the center of the room and stood between the two smoke grenades. His eyes gleamed as he scanned the room, taking in every detail, spotting every nuance, his mind calculating, adjusting, tuning his plan to the reality of what he saw.

He raised his assault rifle and fired a three-round warning burst, punching a tight pattern of bullet holes in a ceiling tile. Hostages screamed and clutched each other. Aaron's ears rang, and he watched, mesmerized, as bits of white fluff drifted down through the blue smoke like the artificial snowflakes at a winter-theme dance.

The gunman tipped his fedora back slightly. "Okay, people!" he shouted, his pace rapid-fire. "We don't have a lot of time or technology. So listen up!" Wildly charismatic, the man made a very strong impression, and though they couldn't see his face, several female hostages found themselves strangely attracted to him.

"When I say 'go,' my friend and I will do the following ... to this entire fucking bank!"

Aaron felt a bolt of adrenaline arc through him and he held his breath.

The man put his rifle to his hip and fired a quick burst, cutting three loan-approval desktops neatly off. Wood chips littered the area as echoes of rifle fire faded into horrified silence.

"Do I make myself clear?" he said, and judging by the reaction, he had.

The man in neon-green walked over and stood back-to-back with him, their rifles forming a black X. Aaron scrambled over and crouched low next to them. Thick blue smoke swirled about the brightly masked trio, adding to the surrealism of the moment.

The man in electric-blue tipped his fedora forward and started the count.

"*Ready ... ?*"

Aaron (deaf in both ears after the first shots) covered his ears tightly with his hands.

"*Set ... !*"

The hostages watched, breathless.

"*Go!*"

The trigger men grit their teeth and fired low, burning streams of bullets, sawing everything waist high in half as they circled to their left. Hostages screamed and dove for cover as death passed overhead in a hail of debris.

Within seconds the men completed a full circle and ceased fire. A metallic ringing sound reverberated about the lobby, then abruptly died, as dust, smoke, and the sweet smell of gunpowder filled the room.

John Avery

- PART ONE -

AARON QUINN

John Avery

-WEDNESDAY-

Two Days Earlier ...

John Avery

Chapter 2

ALL IN GOOD FUN

Report from the *Daily Tribune*, 12 March 1905:

DOZENS DIE IN WATERFRONT CANNERY EXPLOSION

The Alton Brothers Fish Cannery was destroyed by fire yesterday evening during a night-shift of over 200 employees. It was determined that a faulty pressure-relief valve, deemed safe by the deputy engineer, caused the cannery's coal-fired boiler to explode. The force of the blast set off a chain of secondary explosions and fires that ran through the building, causing the entire structure, along with one hundred and forty-seven trapped workers, to collapse and burn to the ground. The deputy engineer was later found dead in his home after an apparent suicide.

"Ahem!" she bellowed, using as much authority in her voice as she could muster.

Aaron Quinn's head jerked up from the table, and for a moment he thought the knives behind his eyes had severed his optic nerves. Instinctively he reached out a hand then recoiled in disgust as his fingers squished into something like warm cheese in a knit sack.

He blinked, grossed out. There in front of him, so close she blocked his view of the middle-school library like the side of a bus, stood the evening's billowy on-duty teacher.

She looked down aghast at the fold in her stomach where Aaron's fingers had blundered, then gave him a look that curled his toes and trundled back to her office, longing for the good-old-days when she would have taught the audacious punk a quick lesson in the use of hardwood.

Aaron wiped his hand on his jeans then checked the large clock on the wall across the room. 7:29 p.m. He had managed to sleep through nearly all three hours of detention.

He unzipped his sweatshirt. The air-circulator had shut down at the end of the normal school day and the library was hot and airless, as if the countless thousands of books and magazines surrounding him lived on oxygen. He did a few neck rolls to ease the tension in his shoulders, then drained his water bottle and squashed it flat.

Laid open on the table in front of him was a large, leather-bound book: *Strange Disasters of the 20th Century* – a collection of bizarre newspaper articles from the 1900s.

A small puddle of drool was soaking into a photograph from the article he'd been reading before he fell asleep. A gruesome image, the old photo showed the many dozens of contorted bodies that had yet to be extricated from the ashes of the 1905 cannery fire.

Aaron pulled the sleeve of his sweat-shirt down over the heel of his hand and wiped the offending spot dry, taking a moment to reread the last sentence of the article. He paused over the word *suicide* before closing the heavy book and returning it to its home on the shelf behind him.

He looked across to the far side of the library at his co-

conspirator (seated as far from him as the proportions of the space would allow), Wilson "Willy" Abbott, a short (shorter than Aaron, at least, who was considered short for his age), round, black kid with big hands, a blinding smile, and stout glasses. Willy would have exchanged Aaron's glance if he could see that far.

Willy lived near Aaron – one minute by bicycle – in the same crumbling neighborhood in downtown's west-side. They had met the first day of first-grade when poor little Willy couldn't find his classroom. Aaron had seen the boy wandering the halls like a duckling separated from its mother and had offered to help him out, comparing his and Willy's schedules. "Room 5 – Mrs. White," he had read. "What do you know? We're in the same class." Aaron liked the kid with the big teeth and the British accent, and the two started to hang out. They'd been best friends ever since.

Brrrinnnggg! The late-bell signaled the end of detention and the release of the two detainees. Aaron and Willy grabbed their packs and fled the library through a side door.

It was a cold, blustery evening outside, and to Aaron, after a long afternoon in the stuffy library, the air felt fresh and wonderful. The boys crossed the lawn by the gym in near darkness and headed for the front of the school – Aaron taking the straighter path, while Willy dodged around trees and hurdled bushes like one of Robin Hood's men eluding pursuit in Sherwood Forest.

"Detention sucks," Willy said, jumping down from the top of a high stone wall. "One lousy prank and you'd think we were a couple of blaggers whipping out Uzis in a bank lobby."

Aaron laughed, picturing the two of them, with masks and

machine guns, robbing a bank like a couple of eighth-grade hooligans.

"It wasn't just a prank, you know," he said. "We ditched the whole first day of school!" He felt guilty about ditching (this being his first time), but only slightly. Each year his teachers seemed less and less interested in him, and the further he and the educational system drifted apart, the more difficult it became for him to return. So this year when Willy ditched the first day (as he did every year), Aaron ditched, too.

"And don't forget the forged permission slips," Willy added proudly, clearing a long concrete bench from end to end, a surprisingly agile move, considering the extra inches he carried around his middle.

"Oh, yeah," Aaron agreed. "Those, too." Willy's fake documents hadn't worked, but it was a commendable effort.

"All in good fun," Willy said cheerfully.

They crossed the middle-school's broad central plaza under a golden canopy of autumn leaves, and exited through the main gate, their sneakers tapping out a random rhythm on the polished granite as they descended the wide front steps.

Across the boulevard from the middle-school stood Community Plaza Bank, a stately structure with a marble colonnade echoing a classic Greek temple, and a pair of grand, plate-glass front doors. Community Plaza was the largest and busiest bank in the city, but neither Aaron nor Willy had ever been inside.

Aaron checked the huge clock mounted on its towering facade and the stabbing pain behind his eyes returned with a vengeance.

"I am *so* dead," he said gloomily, his throat tightening at the thought of going home and facing Tom.

Willy knew that Aaron's stepdad did not tolerate rebellious behavior, and that the man wasn't the least bit squeamish when it came to tough discipline.

"I'm starving," he said. "You want to get a burger?"

"Tom would love that," Aaron said bitterly. "Unlike you, I can't come and go as I please."

To Willy that comment felt cold, considering he had no parents at all. His mother, born and raised in England, had given birth to him at the age of fifteen while living in south London, and had never told the father. At the age of twenty, she died of alcohol poisoning, leaving Willy an orphan. His grieving grandparents took him in, and together they immigrated to the United States. Willy's father would later be awarded the Victoria Cross for bravery while serving in Iraq as a commando in the British Royal Marines, but unfortunately Willy never heard about this, because he and his father never met.

"Maybe tomorrow then, mate?" he said, but Aaron was lost in thought and didn't answer.

The tubular-steel bike rack was bolted to the sidewalk next to the street, its undulating pipes shaped to spell the word SCHOOL. Aaron had parked his old BMX bike in the letter H, next to the O that held Willy's rusty beach cruiser.

Aaron knelt and tried his lock, but it was stuck. Willy removed his own lock with ease, then stuffed it in his pack and pulled his bike out of the O.

Aaron gave his lock a swift kick. The lock banged hard against the bike frame, but didn't open.

"Stupid piece-of-crap!" he yelled, giving the lock another hard kick. This time the lock opened, and he nearly broke the rack yanking his bike out of the H.

To Willy's surprise, Aaron looped his pack over his shoulder, swung a leg over his bike, and rudely pedaled off down the street without him.

Willy watched him for a moment, uncertain whether or not to follow, then set off to eat his dinner alone.

Chapter 3

SLEEPING DOGS

It was completely dark as Aaron rode alone toward home. He knew he'd been cruel to his friend, leaving him like he did, and he felt awful. But he couldn't help himself. He was pissed off at the world. Taking advantage of Willy's good nature was easier than being the good friend he deserved. He looked back a couple of times, hoping to see Willy, but there was no one there.

Suddenly he heard the unmistakable click of dog paws approaching at a full sprint. A large Rottweiler sleeping in a side alley had awakened to the tantalizing grind of bicycle tires on pavement and given chase – and it was closing on him. His heart fell into his shoes, and he wished he'd taken Willy up on his burger offer.

Instinctively, Aaron accelerated, but a quick look back convinced him that it was futile, and judging by the size and look of the dog, he knew he was in serious trouble.

An article he had read online flashed into his mind: It had said that in the event of a dog attack while riding a bike, dismount and use your bike as a shield, and if it came down to pure survival, to jam your arm down the attacking dog's throat, choking it to death.

I'm not sure I could do that, he thought wretchedly.

But he had no time to consider his options – the dog was upon him. He said a quick prayer, hit the brakes, leaped off his bike, and swung it around between himself and a horrible fate.

The vicious animal lunged at him repeatedly, barking its lungs out, as if its very survival depended upon its ability to catch and eat teenage boys. Aaron fought desperately, dodging the dog's enormous head, as again and again the animal thrust snarling, snapping jaws full of huge, foaming teeth through the gaps in his bike frame.

He battled on, somehow managing to keep his bike between them, until finally – after what felt like an eternity – the dog tired and just stood in the street panting. It looked at Aaron with its head cocked, as if to say *Shit, man ... I didn't expect that much fight from someone your size.* Then, at last, having lost interest, it trotted off into the darkness.

For a couple of minutes Aaron couldn't move. He cowered behind his bike, soaked to the skin with sweat, his hands shaking and sticky with strings of dog snot. He struggled to get a grip on himself as the terrifying event played over and over, in exquisitely painful detail, in his mind.

He looked back down the street to make sure the dog had gone, then, still trembling, rode nervously on toward home, grateful that he wasn't forced to try the arm-down-the-throat trick.

Chapter 4

DINNER FOR THREE

Aaron hauled his bike up the cracked concrete steps of the aging two-story red-brick townhouse and bumped his way through the door to his home.

He kicked the door closed behind him, and as he went to lean his bike against a wall he caught his reflection in the hall mirror and his heart fell – add a red waistband and neckerchief and he was one of the unlucky runners at the *encierro* in Pamplona.

He jumped when his mother called to him from the dining room.

"*Aaron, sweetie ... ? Is that you?*"

"*Coming ...*" he coughed, then used his sleeve to wipe the dirt and sweat from his face. He attempted to straighten his matted hair, then sucked in a deep breath, pulled his lips back into something resembling a smile, and entered the dining room.

The small dining table was covered with a crisp, white cloth and set for three. Aaron took his regular seat in the middle of one side, trying his best to appear normal.

Seated at the end to his right, his mother, Ashley Quinn, served him a beautifully prepared plate of food – a trick, considering she had stalled dinner for nearly an hour.

To Aaron's left, at the head of the table, sat his stepdad of four months, Thomas Davidson. During the four long years following the death of her husband, Daniel Quinn, Ashley had not re-married, or even dated, believing that no man could replace Aaron's father. Eventually, however, she met and married Tom – a decision that she and Aaron had lived to regret.

Tom hadn't spoken a word since Aaron arrived, silence being one of his preferred methods of torture.

Aaron cast about frantically for a plausible excuse for being late for dinner; but his stomach was sick and his head was spinning, so he came up empty. He picked up his fork and poked his potatoes.

"So, how was school?" Ashley asked brightly, attempting to lighten the somber mood. It was obvious that Aaron had been in some kind of trouble, but she didn't want to say anything in front of Tom.

Aaron watched with dismay as his dinner moved about the plate like a food commercial directed by Salvador Dali. He glanced up at the question, then back at his surreal plate of food, clearing his throat carefully to avoid puking on his peas.

"It was okay," he managed, praying he sounded better to them than he did to himself.

"Go ahead, then," Ashley said. "Eat your dinner while it's still warm."

"Sorry I'm late," Aaron said, glancing at Tom. Then he forgot what he was going to say and had to ad lib. "I was at the library and lost track of time." *Well, that certainly sucked*, he thought miserably.

Tom poured gravy over a slice of steak then stabbed it with

his fork and slid it between his teeth. A moist, brown dribble worked its way down through the stubble on his chin.

"That's it?" he said. "That's the best you could come up with?"

Aaron's white lie was all he had. What good would it do to tell Tom about detention? Or the dog? He wouldn't understand. He was on *their* side.

Tom washed the masticated meat down with cheap Scotch, then leaned forward in his chair and changed the subject.

"I got a call today from the manager of the Community Plaza Bank downtown," he said, sending a cloud of bad air Aaron's way. "We need to be there before they open for business in the morning to fix a broken toilet."

"But I've got school tomorrow," Aaron said.

"I know," Tom said. "I've got a business to run, and I need your help."

Aaron clenched his teeth, unable to speak. He couldn't miss any more school. No way. Not after ditching the whole first day and with detention and everything ... He looked to his mother for support.

She looked back at him sympathetically, then turned to Tom. "Aaron really shouldn't miss any –"

Tom slammed an open hand on the table. "Did I *ask* for your opinion? I don't think I did."

Ashley's cheeks flushed with embarrassment, but she remained composed for her son's sake.

An angry scream rose in Aaron's throat, but he fought it down. He'd been on the receiving end of Tom's abuse plenty of times, but to hear it directed at his mother was too much.

He gripped the tablecloth, trying not to tremble, and spoke forcibly. "Don't talk to my mother like that," he said, bracing himself.

Tom looked at him like gum on his shoe. "What?" he said.

Aaron hesitated. "I said –"

"Shut up," Tom said, cutting him off with a pointed finger. "I'll deal with you later."

He turned back to Ashley.

Aaron stood up from the table and looked squarely at him. "I wish my father was alive and you were dead!" Then, with a quick glance at his mother he headed for the front door.

Ashley stood and threw her napkin at Tom, then ran after her son, making a solemn promise that before the night was through, Tom would be out of their lives forever.

She ran to the sidewalk and checked the street, but Aaron was gone.

Chapter 5

THE HIDEOUT

Tears washed over Aaron's face as he pedaled his bike south through the downtown neighborhoods. He rode hard, flying on and off sidewalks, jumping railroad tracks, potholes, and puddles, gulping the crisp night air, his heart in his throat, feeling as if he could explode with tension. He rode to lose himself in the anonymity of the city, to shake off the weight bearing down on him, to mute the angry voices shouting at him from within his aching head.

He passed endless rows of apartment buildings, some with lighted windows behind which he pictured families having dinner or watching TV by the fire. He wondered how many of the families were happy and how many were as messed up as his, and he seriously considered stopping and knocking on a few doors to see if any of the households were functioning smoothly enough to take in a feral teenager.

At last he arrived at his destination: the city's waterfront, the dominion of the criminally inclined and the criminally insane. He skidded to a stop under a mercury-vapor streetlamp that cast a tawny light upon a vast cliff of rusting corrugated-steel siding the length of a city block, The Alton Brothers Fish Cannery – aka the hideout. Rebuilt in 1907 following the 1905 fire, the cannery had been in operation for more than a hundred years before it was condemned in the mid 1990s.

Aaron took a couple of slow, deep breaths. His head still hurt, but the pain in his stomach was easing a bit. He took out his cell phone and fired off a text message.

Willy was working on his second cheeseburger when his phone beeped. It was a text from Aaron:

I'm at the cannery. Can you come down?

Willy rubbed his nose and read the message again – neither one of them had been down to the hideout in months, and he had assumed that Aaron had gone home mad. He glanced at the clock on the restaurant wall and entered his reply:

It's past your bedtime you big baby.

Aaron laughed and texted Willy back:

I couldn't sleep. Are you coming or not?

Willy took the last bite of his burger, washed it down with his drink, and thumbed in his reply:

Okay, Boss. I'm coming.

Aaron smiled and pocketed his phone. He had loved Willy as a friend over the years not simply because he was innocent, fun loving, and loyal (Willy would cut off an arm for Aaron), but because Willy was crazy; he was Aaron's alter-ego – the Mr. Hyde to his Dr. Jekyll. Willy encouraged Aaron to do things he would never do on his own, to act in ways unnatural to his shy, withdrawn personality. Willy liberated Aaron from himself, and Aaron was addicted to Willy like a drug.

This year, for instance, the boys had first-period biology together, and their teacher – in addition to being a jerk – was missing the thumb on his right hand. "This guy's a bit of a wanker," Willy had concluded (he was fairly well

Americanized by then, but occasionally the British slang he picked up from his grandfather slipped out). So, whenever either of them raised their hand to ask a question, they folded their thumb in, and when the teacher was out of the room, Willy might hold up four fingers and make an announcement like, *Attention class! You have five minutes to finish your test!* In fact, Willy was so highly skilled, he was easily capable of sending Aaron, along with an entire classroom full of students, into fits of uncontrollable laughter whenever the urge struck, and laughter was something Aaron craved, something he wished he could do more of, especially at home.

Willy dumped his trash in the nearest receptacle, grabbed his pack, and walked out of the restaurant. His beach cruiser was locked to a pole by the entrance; he unlocked it, strapped his pack to his back, hopped aboard, and stomped the pedals.

Aaron felt around on the cannery's steel siding and found their secret entrance: a loose panel to the right of the large, steel roll-up door (retrofitted in 1965) that opened into the main warehouse. He pulled the panel open and ducked inside, dragging his bike behind him.

Slatted light from the streetlamp lit a cavernous space filled with the dusty conveyors, tables and miscellaneous machinery of a once thriving fish-packing business. The familiar smell of fish guts still hung in air, and Aaron wondered why after all this time – the cannery had been closed for years – it had not gone away. He also noticed that it was unseasonably warm, hot even, but it didn't seem important so he let it go.

He leaned his bike against a post and unzipped his

sweatshirt, then threaded his way through the junk maze until he came to the back of the building and a flight of rough, wooden stairs which he ascended to the second floor.

He stepped off the landing onto the long, wood-planked balcony that led to the cannery's office. On his immediate right was a steel door marked MAINTENANCE; he opened it and stepped inside, closing the door behind him.

He felt around in the dark for the candle and lighter he and Willy had left on a shelf months ago, and as he lit the candle, two mice, startled by the flame, took off in opposite directions and disappeared.

The small space was packed with the essentials of building maintenance: tools, cleaning products, old buckets of paint, wire – all blanketed with a thick layer of dust. Aaron brushed the cobwebs aside and made his way to a large, unpainted, wooden cabinet in the back of the room. He opened the cabinet doors and pulled an old tweed suitcase out from the bottom shelf. He laid it on the floor, then knelt next to it and flipped open the latches.

The case was stocked with basic hideout necessities: a stack of comics, some playing cards, a spare candle and matches. Beneath the stack of comics was a small, royal-blue satin box. Aaron lifted the little box from the suitcase and held it in his hands for a moment, then opened the lid.

Inside was a small photo; he picked it up and held it toward the light.

It was a one-of-a-kind shot of his mother hugging his real father, Daniel Quinn. Aaron had taken the picture himself with a disposable camera during a family vacation while his dad was home on furlough the summer before he was killed in action overseas. Taken in an alpine meadow just before sunset when the light was perfect – the priceless photo represented the last days they spent together as a family; and whenever his heart was heavy, Aaron turned his thoughts to that wonderful summer. He took a moment, then carefully tucked the dog-eared picture into his wallet.

Suddenly Aaron heard the sound of footsteps coming up the stairs to the second floor. A chill ran through him – it wasn't Willy in his sneakers. It sounded more like two or three men in leather-soled shoes. He quickly slid the case onto its shelf, and closed the cabinet. Then he held his breath as the footsteps crossed the stair landing and moved past the maintenance room toward the office at the end of the balcony.

He blew out the candle, then crept to the door and opened it a crack, in time to see three large men in business suits file into the office, leaving the door slightly ajar. Aaron stayed where he was and listened.

Chapter 6

A CLUMSY FOOL

Johnny Souther removed his leather fedora and dropped two bags of fast food onto an immense oak desk piled high with books and magazines. He lit a gasoline lantern – the city had cut the electricity to the cannery building when it was condemned a few years back – then sat behind the desk. The other two pulled up wooden chairs and faced him.

Souther grabbed a cheeseburger from one of the bags and unwrapped it. But instead of eating the sandwich, he simply held it in his hands and looked at it. He had spent half of the last ten years eating similar food off of metal trays while under armed guard, and had never lost his taste for it, but last night's botched bank job had left him without an appetite. He folded the cheeseburger into its wrapper and dropped it back in the bag with the others.

Nearly everyone Souther knew outside prison he had known inside. One of them was the big black man sitting across the desk from him, Benjamin "Beeks" Madison, whom Souther had met while working in a prison laundry.

Beeks was starving, and the smell of the food was killing him. But just as he started to reach for a burger, Souther cranked open the window next to his desk and tossed both bags out into the darkness, then cranked the window shut.

Saliva flooded Beeks's mouth, and a tear came to his eye as he pictured himself enjoying his tasty dinner.

Souther shifted in his chair, his hip joint hurting as the result of letting a security guard shoot him five years before. He knew he couldn't be present at every robbery, and he thought he had put a good man in charge. But last night things had gone terribly wrong, and he deeply regretted not having been there.

He removed a bottle of whiskey and a glass from his desk drawer and poured himself a drink. He tossed the shot back and slammed the glass on the desk, then spoke slowly, in a low, well-worn voice.

"This morning I had five men – eleven, counting the fools doing nickels upstate. And now I have what, *two?* Hell ... Wallace did better at Stirling fucking Bridge."

It wasn't simply the loss of his men that upset Souther; there was also the loss of income (his chief financial burden being his long-time girlfriend, Brandy Fine, a twenty-five-year-old redhead knockout whose extravagant taste for clothes, cars, nice homes, and jet-set travel demanded copious quantities of cash). It helped that the income from his various business ventures was tax-free, but there was never enough.

Lars "Needles" Sheldon had never even considered stepping outside the law until he met Johnny Souther, but with an instinctive flair for the demanding work of a bank robber, he had quickly become one of Souther's most trusted inside men. He leaned back in his chair and ran a hand through his silver hair.

"Diggs should never have let the bank manager into the vault without –"

"Without frisking the fucker first, right?" Souther said,

interrupting Needles. "I know, damn it. If he had, Freddie wouldn't have had his damn head blown off."

"Larry, either," Needles added.

"I know. Shit!" Souther picked up a large hardback book with both hands and slammed it down on his desk, shattering Beeks's nerves in an attempt to calm his own.

Needles was well aware of the importance of frisking bank managers – having uncovered several concealed weapons himself that way. When he was in charge of a job he was meticulous about such matters, but he wasn't in charge on this job – he wasn't even there. Diggs was.

Souther drew a deep breath in through his nose and released it slowly out his mouth. With Diggs looking at life in prison, and all his other men either doing time or dead, Needles and Beeks were all he had. He looked at them sadly, then pulled two more glasses out of his desk and poured them both a drink.

Aaron trembled, terrified, unable to believe what he'd just overheard. He slipped out of the maintenance room and took a few cautious steps toward the stairs. But in the dim light he tripped over a pile of loose steel pipes and tumbled to the floor – making a huge racket.

Souther stood and drew his .45 automatic.

Aaron lay still, holding his breath, his heart bouncing off his ribs like a boxer's speed-bag. He pictured his epitaph, carved in granite:

> Here Lies Young Aaron Quinn
> A Clumsy Fool Until The End

Souther picked up a large black flashlight, clicked it on, then eased the office door open with his foot and stepped slowly out onto the walkway, sighting down the powerful beam with his pistol. Needles and Beeks drew their guns and followed him.

The men worked their way slowly down the long balcony, checking behind stacks of boxes and under piles of junk, moving closer to Aaron with each step.

Icy fingers gripped Aaron's heart as Souther's flashlight sliced through the darkness like a great saber.

Willy rounded the corner in front of the cannery, pedaling his beach cruiser at full speed. He jumped the curb under the mercury-vapor streetlamp and stomped his coaster brake, laying a long black patch of rubber across the wide, concrete sidewalk.

Two vans were parked at the curb – one white, one black. Willy glanced at them curiously. Then, whistling a simple tune, he pulled open the secret panel and pushed his beach cruiser inside.

Willy paused to let his eyes adjust to the darkness, then leaned his bike against Aaron's and worked his way through the junk maze to the back staircase.

He jumped as a bright beam of light swept across the balcony railing above him, but he assumed it was Aaron and started up the stairs.

The three men were practically on top of Aaron.

"If you find the fucker, waste him," Souther said.

Willy heard the strange voice and stopped, then backed slowly down the steps and ducked behind a piece of machinery.

Aaron tried to crawl away, but the loose pipes were everywhere. Souther hit him with the flashlight beam and fired. The concussion nearly burst Aaron's left eardrum, and he cried out as the bullet splintered wood next to his ear.

Willy screamed, but he caught it with his hand and shoved it back into his mouth.

"Don't shoot!" Aaron cried, throwing his hands high in surrender. "I give up!" Tears streamed down his cheeks as he got to his knees. "I'm here! Please, God ... don't shoot."

Willy was horrified, confused, and powerless to help his friend. He said a quick prayer, then closed his eyes tightly and listened, shivering in a state of shock.

Souther kicked a wooden crate to one side and stabbed his light into the eyes of the trembling boy kneeling before him.

"Stand up," he commanded.

Shaking in every limb, Aaron could barely keep his hands raised. He got to his feet and faced his captor. The man towered over him, eyes dark and cold. Deep lines ran down the sides of his face, and Aaron had a stomach lurching sense of the depth of the man's evil.

He didn't see the punch coming; it impacted his face with such force that he was sure it had caved in. His vision and balance left him and he fell sprawling to the floor.

Beeks was shocked. "What was that for?" he said.

Aaron opened his eyes and touched a hand to his face; his fingers came back with blood. He looked up just in time to see Johnny Souther take aim at him with his pistol. Instinctively he held up an arm and turned his head, preparing to die.

Needles grabbed Souther's wrist.

Souther jerked his arm free and turned the gun on him.

Needles stumbled back a step, swallowing his breath. A

drop of sweat dripped off the end of his nose, one inch from the gun barrel. "The boy hasn't done anything," he said.

"He's seen our faces, you idiot," Souther said.

A bolt of pure instinct pierced Aaron's spine, triggering a desperate dash for the stairs. Souther fired. The bullet whizzed past Aaron's head, and with no hesitation he leaped over the second-floor railing and piled into a stack of cardboard boxes fifteen feet below. Souther ran to the railing and looked over, trying to track him with the flashlight.

Aaron quickly found his feet and sprinted across the cannery, passing mere feet from Willy. Souther fired two more shots that ricocheted off the loose siding panel just as Aaron dove through and disappeared into the night.

"Find him," Souther said, fixing Needles with a look of utter contempt. "And don't come back till you do. I'll be damned if I'm going to let some punk roam the city crying about my line of work."

"He won't get far," Needles said, praying that was true.

Willy was frozen in place, his thoughts and heart rate a dizzying blur. Dusty air moved quickly in and out of his lungs as he strained to hear what was happening above him. He watched terrified as Needles and Beeks descended the stairs. Then, as the thugs exited the cannery, he waited, until at last the third pair of leather soled shoes moved away down the balcony toward the office.

He sent a quick text message to Aaron:

Bloody hell! Are you okay? Where are you?

Souther stopped abruptly, then turned and walked back toward the stair landing. Willy tucked his phone away and held his breath.

Aaron's phone lay on the walkway directly above Willy's position. The text message glowed brightly on the small screen.

Souther reached down, picked the phone up off the floor, and read the message. Then he stepped to the railing and sprayed his flashlight beam down into the warehouse. Willy covered his mouth with his hand and made himself smaller as the hot patch of white light swept past his toes.

Souther paused, listening, then clicked off the flashlight and walked back to his office and closed the door.

Willy waited a few moments for his heart to slow, then crawled out from his hiding place, tip toed over to his beach cruiser, and slipped quietly out of the cannery.

Chapter 7

CREEK SIDE PARK

Michael St. John sat hunched over his computer, notes, papers, and books stacked high around him. His writing studio (defined by large bookcases stuffed with research materials) occupied one small corner of an enormous, luxury loft apartment that consumed the entire 4,000 sq ft top floor of a converted four-story Brownstone. After writing his first short story at the age of six, he discovered that he not only loved writing, but according to his first-grade teacher he had a talent for it as well. Now, thirty years later, he was considered a very successful novelist.

It was an arduous task for Michael to reach the depths of concentration necessary to coax his muse out of her robe and slippers, and today was one of those days when it just wasn't going to happen. He scrolled through his manuscript one last time, trying to get flowing again, but his muse simply laughed at him and put another log on the fire.

Frustrated, he highlighted the entire page of manuscript and hit DELETE. Then he stood up from his desk, closed his computer, and walked out the door.

Michael exited his building through the underground garage, walking the steep driveway up to the street. He braced himself against a strong wind and bitter cold and thought about going back for a heavier coat, but he was afraid he'd end up back at the computer, so instead he just pulled up his collar and toughed it out.

As he crossed the street to Creek Side Park (a quaint inner-city park with a year-round stream that was showing signs of icing over), Michael could see the owner of his favorite hot dog and pretzel cart struggling with the cart's umbrella – its red, yellow, and green stripes a muddy blur and the whole thing in danger of helicoptering away in the wind. Michael trotted over and helped him tie the umbrella down, and the grateful man bought him a pretzel.

Michael took a seat on a nearby stone bench, brushed some of the salt from his pretzel, squeezed on a packet of mustard, and took a generous bite.

A rustle in the bushes startled him. He stood and turned toward the sound, swallowing his mouthful whole. Unnerved, he pushed some leaves aside and was surprised to see a boy kneeling in the dirt.

Aaron was still in shock; he wasn't sure where he was or what he was doing there. He tried to crawl away, but a granite wall blocked his escape. Michael caught him by the arm, easily overpowering him.

"Easy there, cowboy," Michael said, lifting Aaron to his feet. "Aren't we a little old for hide-and-seek?"

Aaron was unable to find the humor in that. His mouth and chin were caked with blood, as were the strings of brown hair falling over his eyes. His sweatshirt and jeans were filthy and torn, revealing numerous cuts and bruises. He glanced around wildly, breathing rapidly through his nostrils. A thread of blood flowed from a purple gash across his left cheekbone, and he was very cold.

Michael eased his grip slightly. He could smell sweat, and fear. "What in God's name happened to you?" he said. "You're a mess ... your cheek, it's –"

Aaron turned away and winced in pain as he wiped his face on the sleeve of his sweatshirt, leaving a dark red streak on the gray fabric.

Michael was genuinely concerned for the boy. "Here," he said, gesturing toward the bench. "Sit down for a minute ... It's okay."

Aaron looked around, nervous and frightened, shivering in the icy wind.

Michael saw him glance at his pretzel and said, "You must be starving. Let me get you something to eat. You want a hot dog?"

Aaron didn't answer, but his face said *I'd die for a hot dog.*

Michael helped him to the bench, then removed his jacket and draped it over the boy's shoulders. "Stay right here and don't move," he said. "I'll be back in a flash."

Aaron pulled Michael's jacket in close around him. The bizarre incident in the cannery occurred to him now as a strange, aching nightmare, but in his gut he knew there really was someone after him. He continued to scan the perimeter of the park as he sat alone on the cold, stone bench.

Michael returned carrying a steaming hot dog that overflowed with ketchup, mustard and pickle relish. He took a seat next to Aaron and handed it to him.

"My name's Michael," he said, extending his hand.

Aaron cleared his throat and managed a response. "I'm

Aaron," he said, feeling as if someone else had spoken for him. He shook Michael's hand with a grip that was limp and clammy.

Like a cold, dead fish, Michael thought, discreetly wiping his palm on his pants. It was obvious that the boy had been seriously traumatized.

"I know you're in some kind of trouble, Aaron," he said. "We should give your parents a call."

"*No!*" Aaron said quickly. He wasn't ready for that yet, and besides, Tom might be the one to answer. "My stepdad and I had a fight, okay? And they're not my parents. I mean my mother is – but my real dad died."

Michael knew there was a lot more to the story, but he took Aaron's hint and changed the subject.

"You live around here?" he asked.

Aaron thought for a moment then said honestly, "I'm not sure." Then he picked up the hot dog and bit off as big a bite as the pain in his face would allow, sending the classic American condiments squishing out from the corners of his mouth.

Michael looked over toward his apartment building. At street level, assorted signs identified small businesses that really had no business being in business. One of them had a small, green neon sign that read SALLY'S DINER.

"See that diner over there?" he asked, pointing.

Aaron followed his gaze and nodded.

"I live at the top of that building," Michael said. "Have you ever eaten there? At Sally's, I mean?"

Aaron shook his head and made a face that said *Why would anyone want to? It looks disgusting.*

Michael was amused by his reaction. "If you think Sally's

looks bad," he said, "wait till you see the cook."

Aaron laughed a little, and it felt good. Michael felt better, too, having succeeded in lightening the mood.

"He's actually a nice guy," Michael explained, "and his food is surprisingly good. I say, if you don't get some greasy food in you once in a while – you know, to build your immunity – you'll probably die when you eat some by mistake."

Aaron laughed at the offbeat logic. "I believe that," he said, nodding.

Michael went on. "I work from home, so I end up down at Sally's a lot. Sometimes I go to eat ... sometimes just to relax and get away from my work."

Michael had grown fond of the little diner over the years and to him its faults were its charms. And besides, he couldn't beat the convenience: a two minute walk from his loft – including the elevator ride.

"I'm surprised you don't weigh 600 pounds," Aaron said candidly, picturing a huge version of Michael bulging over a stool at the counter.

Michael laughed then smiled to himself as the boy opened up even more. "Lucky for me my metabolism is still cranked," he said. "I hear that once I hit forty, things will slow down, and Sally and I may have to part company."

Aaron smiled then finished the last few bites of his food with enthusiasm.

Michael tossed their wrappers in a nearby container and wiped his mouth with a napkin.

"Listen," he said. "I know I'm just a stranger, and this may sound a bit weird, but what kind of person would I be if I just sent you off into the night? I have the makings for hot chocolate upstairs and I thought you might be thirsty – and I guarantee it will warm you up."

Aaron thought the hot chocolate idea sounded pretty good. But it *was* kinda weird. It was bad enough to talk to strangers, but to *go home with one?* "Thank you," he said, "but I don't think that's a good idea."

Michael had anticipated Aaron's negative response. "Look," he said, "You have every right to be nervous. But it's okay. I could take a look at those cuts ... and I have an arcade – or we could shoot some pool. Do you like pool?"

Aaron perked at that. He had always wanted to play pool. His real dad had promised to take him to play at the officer's club when he was old enough.

Look at your choices, he thought, glancing around again. *You can sit here on this bench in this park, exposed to the weather, or a shot in the head; or you can go somewhere warm and drink hot chocolate ... and play pool.*

Michael sensed a shift. "A quick drink to warm you up, some first aid – maybe a game of pool, and you're on your way." He put his hands on his knees and sat up expectantly. "What do you say?"

Aaron's only other option was to go home and face Tom, and he considered it for a moment. But he decided his bones were bruised enough already and said, "I guess maybe one game wouldn't hurt."

The white van was parked near Sally's Diner, across the street from Creek Side Park. Needles and Beeks watched in silence as Michael walked Aaron across the street on their way to his loft.

THREE DAYS TO DIE

Chapter 8

THE PERFECT GENTLEMAN

Willy Abbott jumped off his bike and bounded up the steps to Aaron's apartment – leaving his beach cruiser to ghost down the block a few yards, where it bounced off a bus bench and crashed to the sidewalk.

Fortunately for Willy, Tom had long since passed out, and Aaron's mom answered the doorbell. Willy did a double take – he hadn't seen Aaron's mom in a while and had forgotten how pretty she was. He noticed a bruise below her right eye that she'd obviously tried to cover with makeup.

"Hello, Mrs. Quinn," he said. "Aaron's not home by any chance, is he?"

"Oh – hi, Willy," she said, looking past him into the street. "I was hoping he was with you. He left on his bike during dinner and hasn't come home."

She checked her watch. 9:45 p.m.

"I'm starting to worry," she said, and then her heart was lifted by an idea. "What about your grandparents? Maybe they've heard from him."

Willy shook his head sadly. "Sorry, Mrs. Quinn," he said. "They wouldn't know it if Aaron walked in the house and sat on the couch with them."

Ashley cringed. "I'm sorry, Willy," she said. "Aaron never

tells me anything."

Willy wasn't surprised – Aaron never told him anything either.

"I'd better go," he said. "I'm sure he'll show up." He was fibbing about the last part, but he hoped like everything it was true. He turned and trotted down the steps.

I hope you're right, Ashley said to herself, watching him leave. She liked Willy – he was always the perfect little gentleman. She called after him. "If you see him, send him home right away, okay?"

"Will do," Willy said, then with a little wave, "Good night, Mrs. Quinn."

Chapter 9

GRAN CAVALLO

The ancient, cage-style freight-elevator rattled its way toward the top floor of Michael's apartment building. Aaron grinned as pipes and cables rushed past his face, giving him an exhilarating sense of speed.

"This old elevator sold me on the property," Michael said. "My dad had one in the mill where he worked, and he'd let me ride it whenever I visited."

The cage jerked to a stop. Michael pulled on an oiled leather strap, raising the wooden gate that served as a door.

The elevator opened onto a spacious rooftop garden and a long, brick walkway canopied by a yachting-blue awning hung on heavy, polished-brass arches. The walkway was flanked by stone benches and large pots full of fresh flowers and lead to an exquisite pair of huge, hand-tooled copper doors.

Aaron stopped to check them out. The doors depicted a magnificent horse.

"That's Leonardo Da Vinci's *Gran Cavallo*," Michael explained, "the magnificent, twenty-four foot high clay equestrian model he completed in 1492. I found the doors in Milan and had them shipped back here by boat."

"I can't believe I've never heard of that," Aaron said, running his fingers over the highly detailed copper relief. He had read many accounts of Da Vinci's life, but none had mentioned this.

"It's an amazing story," Michael said. "The Gran Cavallo was one of Da Vinci's greatest and most unknown masterpieces. Seventy tons of bronze were set aside for the casting of that horse, but before De Vinci could use it, the precious bronze was sent off and used to make cannons. Then, in 1499, during France's invasion of Italy, French archers used Leonardo's beautiful clay model for target practice, dashing Da Vinci's hope of ever having it cast in bronze, and breaking his heart in the process."

He keyed in the entry alarm code and invited Aaron into his loft with a chivalrous bow and wave of his arm.

"That's an unbelievable story," Aaron said as he stepped through the doors. "To have something that is such a huge part of your life destroyed like that. It's sad."

Michael could relate. "It's very sad," he agreed.

Chapter 10

THE LOFT

Aaron's eyes went wide; never in his wildest dreams had he imagined living anywhere as cool as Michael's outrageous loft apartment. He stood in the entry area craning up at the high ceilings and admiring the eclectic blend of fine original artwork mixed with movie and exotic-car posters.

Next to him, from high in the rafters, a broad sheet of clear water flowed down the face of a polished travertine wall before disappearing into the floor. He poked his finger into the silvery fluid, creating a tiny arcing wave.

The loft was heated to a comfortable temperature. Michael carefully lifted his jacket from Aaron's shoulders and laid it over a chair.

"Take a look around," he said. "The hardwood floors and ceilings are original to the building, but the rest is mine. Oh, and if you need to use the restroom, there are three to choose from." He indicated the doors, each in a separate corner of the loft, then walked over to the kitchen to start a kettle of water.

Aaron didn't know where to begin. In one corner of the enormous space was a classic arcade with pinball machines, console video games, a bowling machine, a dartboard, a chessboard, candy and drink vending machines, and in honor of 21st century technology, a replica 1950s era jukebox with 100 CD capacity, iPod jack, and surround-sound speakers.

Another area was outfitted as a gym, with a basketball hoop (with regulation key), a full-size trampoline, a weight machine, a treadmill, a stationary-bike, and a weight-bench surrounded by free-weights.

In a far corner, Michael had set up a music studio equipped with a dozen vintage guitars and amps, a pro drum kit, and an array of keyboards. The digital recording console had an immense, automated mixing board and was fitted with a pair of the biggest display monitors Aaron had ever seen.

"Your loft ... it's incredible!" he said.

Michael smiled and nodded – he was proud of his success.

He washed and dried his hands then removed a first aid kit from a drawer, opened it, and laid a few items out on the large granite island. "Come on over and sit down for a second," he said. "But wash your hands first."

As Aaron washed up, he found scratches on the backs of his hands that he hadn't noticed under all of the grime. *Damn dog*, he thought, as a brief, frightening image of the manic animal jumped in and out of his mind. Then he took a seat on a stool by the island.

Michael cleaned Aaron's cuts and abrasions and applied antiseptic, gauze and tape. "That should do the trick," he said.

Aaron stood, feeling renewed. He smiled at Michael, grateful for the man's kindness.

While Michael straightened up his mess, Aaron walked across the loft to a wall of glass that provided a spectacular view of the city. He could see Creek Side Park and the post lanterns sparkling off the icy water flowing in the stream. In the distance he could see the Community Plaza Bank building and the lights in his middle-school parking lot.

Michael walked over to a cozy sitting area carrying a tray with two cups of hot chocolate. "Have a seat and help yourself," he said, gesturing toward the sofa. He set the tray on the large ottoman and returned to the kitchen.

Aaron sank into the glove-soft leather, then laid his head back and closed his eyes for a moment. The day's disturbing events simmered in his skull like beef stew over an open fire, blending together into a thick broth, no single event standing out from the rest. He opened his eyes and leaned forward to hook his finger into a cup of chocolate, then took a cautious sip of the steaming beverage.

Michael returned with some brownies and napkins and sat down in an overstuffed chair. "I'm sorry to hear about your father," he said.

Aaron nodded politely. "I was nine when he died," he said. "He was killed while serving in Afghanistan." He couldn't help but recall that dreadful night four years earlier when the doorbell rang: It was around midnight, and he and his mother had both been asleep. He'd been too young to understand why she held his hand so tightly as they walked down the stairs to answer the door. He remembered the look on her face when she saw the notifying officer and the medic. The despair in her eyes. The loneliness. The terror. She had known why they had come.

"I'm very sorry," Michael said.

Aaron took a bite of brownie and grinned, revealing a row of chocolate teeth. "These brownies are amazing," he mumbled.

"You can thank the bakery counter," Michael said.

Aaron chuckled and took another bite.

"Are you ready to shoot some eight-ball?" Michael asked.

He stood and walked over to his custom-made, tournament-size table. "I always say, if you want to feel normal, do something normal."

"Okay," Aaron said, wiping his mouth and hands with a napkin. "What's eight-ball?"

"Don't tell me you've never played pool before," Michael said as he filled the rack with balls.

Aaron didn't say anything.

"Well, it's time you learned," Michael said.

Aaron came over and picked up the glossy cue ball, then rolled it across the table's smooth blood-red baize. It careened off three cushions and came to rest inches from his hand. He marveled at the mysterious physics at work and thought of the pioneering mathematicians who wrote the first theorems defining it.

Suddenly a different image popped into Aaron's head.

"Shit," he said – a word meant for himself, but accidentally spoken out loud.

"Pardon?" Michael said.

"Oh, sorry," Aaron said. "I just remembered something important I forgot to do." He searched his pockets for his phone, but it was missing. He figured he must have dropped it back at the cannery.

"Uh ... Michael?" he said. "May I use your phone?"

Michael nodded. "It's in my jacket, there on the chair."

Aaron found the phone and walked over to the kitchen to make a call.

Willy lay on his bed at home, trying to read. His phone rang with an unfamiliar ringtone, but he picked up anyway.

"Willy, it's Aaron."

Willy instantly sat up, dropping his book. "Where the bleeding hell are you?" he said. "I've been looking all over creation for you. Whose number is this?"

"I – uh ... I'm at a friend's house," Aaron said, glancing at Michael.

"Why didn't you text me back?" Willy demanded. "Do you even know I came down to the cannery to see you? Like you asked me to?"

"I lost my phone and – wait ... You came? When? Was I there?"

"Bloody hell yes, you were there!" Willy said, growing more upset as they talked. He grabbed a pencil from his night table and twirled it nervously through his fingers. "Who's your new friend?"

"Did you see what happened to me?" Aaron asked.

"Of course I did, you wanker! I saw the whole blasted thing! Why aren't you at home?"

"I – uh, I got sidetracked."

Willy paused for a moment, close to losing it. "So, who's your new friend?"

"Oh, he's just a man I met at the park. He's –"

"A *man?* What man? And you're at his house? At night? Are you off your trolley?"

"His name's Michael. He helped me after the –"

"Good for him. So you're headed home now, right?"

"Well – uh ... not yet. We're starting a game of pool. You should see his loft, Willy."

"*Damn it*, Aaron. Who the hell does this Michael guy think he is?"

"*Hey!*" Aaron snapped with sudden viciousness. His temper was short after what he'd been through tonight. "I don't have to take crap from *you* or anyone else, okay? I'll explain everything tomorrow on the way to school – and in the mean time, you can just *chill the hell out!*"

Willy felt like he'd been struck by a fist and was unable to speak for a few moments.

"What's with you, Aaron?" he said at last, his voice as empty as he felt. "It's me ... Willy ... your best friend, remember? Did you at least call your mom? She's worried sick, you know. I was over there earlier, and she's not doing too well."

Aaron *had* forgotten about his mother, but he could no longer be bothered with the trifles of family life. After all, he had escaped being eaten by a dog, then nearly shot and killed, and now he was playing pool in a cool loft – like a man. He felt strong ... independent ... *invincible.*

"Tell someone who cares," he said, his tone cold as an ice axe.

Willy felt as if an artery had been severed. With one unbelievably cruel remark, Aaron had effectively ended their conversation – and their lifelong friendship.

"Screw you, you arrogant son-of-a-bitch," he said.

Aaron was unfazed. "I gotta go," he said.

Willy kept the phone to his ear, but he couldn't speak. Tears came.

"See you tomorrow, Willy," Aaron said with a detached air. He ended the call, then walked over and returned Michael's phone to where he found it.

Michael couldn't help but overhear. "What was that all about?" he asked.

"Oh, nothing," Aaron replied. "Just dealing with an old friend."

Willy tossed his phone on the night table and punched his pillow. "Screw you, Aaron Quinn," he said. "You can just bugger the hell off!" He lay back, pulled his blanket up over his head and cried.

Chapter 11

EIGHT-BALL AND HOUSE CATS

Michael went over the rules for the game of eight-ball. Then he selected two cue sticks from a rack and handed one to Aaron. "That should be a good weight for you," he said. "Go ahead and break."

Aaron's body hurt him as he stretched out over his opening shot (the cardboard boxes hadn't completely broken his fall), but still he managed to drop the 10 ball on the break.

"Nice shooting," Michael said. "You're a natural." But he could see that Aaron was in his own world.

Michael recalled a story. "I have to tell you about this old lady I saw, yesterday," he began. "She was pushing a wheelbarrow down the street with a cat riding in it."

Aaron pocketed the 9 ball.

"And this was the biggest damn cat I've ever seen! I mean this dude was *big!* It was raining hard, and the old lady was trying to hold an umbrella over both herself and the cat; but it wasn't working, and the cat was soaked to the skin."

Aaron followed with the 15 ball.

"But he didn't care one bit. He just rode along, minding his own business, as though it were his daily routine. It was the weirdest thing I've ever seen."

Aaron banked the 12 into the corner pocket, and then leaned on his cue stick and looked at Michael.

"I almost got blown away tonight, you know," he said out of the blue.

Michael was still laughing about the cat. "Uh ... what?" he said.

"Down at the old cannery near the wharf. Some filthy bank robber bastard tried to kill me."

"You've got to be kidding," Michael said, taking a seat on a nearby stool.

"I told you about my fight with my stepdad," Aaron said. "Well, that was true – but he didn't give me this." He pointed to his split cheek, then proceeded to tell Michael the rest of the story.

Chapter 12

HE'S A PSYCHO

Michael ran a hand through his hair. "My God, Aaron," he said, "I don't know what to say." He had never even *made up* a story as wild as the one Aaron had just told him. He stood and walked over to get his phone.

Aaron new immediately what Michael was planning to do. "You're calling the cops, right?" he said. "No way. No cops."

Michael looked at him. "You do know that this low-life scum will come looking for you."

"What, do you think I'm an idiot?" Aaron said. "I know, okay?" Tears welled in his eyes and he stood and walked over to the wall of windows. His face reflected in the glass as he looked out at the city lights and calmed himself for a few moments. "You don't know this man. He's some kind of psycho. If I turn him in, God only knows what he'd do to my mom." He paused. "I can't let that happen."

Michael foolishly hadn't considered that. He replaced his phone, then walked over and stood with Aaron at the window.

"Aaron, I'm sorry," he said. "What's your mother's name?"

Aaron rubbed his nose and spoke softly. "It's Ashley."

"Don't worry, Aaron. I'd never do anything that could hurt Ashley."

Chapter 13

THE ASTON

Michael cast around for a way to change the subject. After a moment he said, "Do you like cars?"

Aaron smiled and wiped his eyes with the backs of his fingers. "I love cars," he replied.

"Follow me," Michael said. "I have something I want to show you." Then he led Aaron down to the underground parking garage.

The garage floor glistened with moisture, and the sound of dripping water could be heard echoing in the distance. Michael and Aaron walked past two dozen vehicles of every class and description parked in neat rows. At the end of the garage, in a space tucked away from the others, they stopped next to a tungsten silver Aston Martin DBS.

Aaron's jaw dropped. "Oh my gosh ... This is yours?"

Michael held out his wrist to Aaron. "Touch your finger here," he said, indicating the little OPEN zone between eight and nine o'clock on his transponder chronograph wristwatch.

Aaron stared at the exquisite marvel of miniaturization.

"A light touch is all it takes," Michael said.

Aaron touched his fingertip to the face of the titanium watch, and the Aston unlocked itself and its dazzling electronics sparkled to life.

"Oh my gosh!" Aaron said. "That is crazy."

"Hop in," Michael said.

Aaron opened the passenger door then hesitated, knowing he was breaking another cardinal rule; then he slid into the low-slung seat.

He looked around the interior, running his hands over the hand-stitched leather and carbon-fiber accents. "This car is unbelievable," he said. "Aren't these like 300 grand or something?"

"'Saturday Night Crash' – Have you seen that?" Michael asked.

"I loved that movie," Aaron replied.

Michael gave the steering wheel a little pat. "I can thank that movie for this car."

Aaron cocked his head, puzzled.

"I wrote it – the book, I mean," Michael said. "My novel was adapted into the movie."

"No way!" Aaron said. "That's *very* cool. You know, I'm thinking about becoming a writer, too."

Michael smiled, but he had heard it a million times. It seemed that nearly everyone he talked to was either trying to become a writer or had thought about it.

"That's a worthy goal," he said finally. "My advice would be to read every day and write every day – and write for the love of writing, or you'll never be able to do the necessary work."

Aaron deflated a little.

"Maybe you and I could talk more about it sometime," Michael said, looking at him.

Aaron smiled. "That'd be great."

Michael fired up the DBS's sweetly tuned engine. "But for

now, let's get you home."

From his seat behind the wheel of the white van, Needles saw the silver Aston Martin exit the underground garage and head west. It passed under a street lamp and he recognized the boy in the passenger seat. Then he pulled away from the curb to follow.

Michael hit the gas for a few seconds to give Aaron a feel for the V-12's awesome power. Aaron giggled and held on. Needles struggled to keep pace, while at the same time trying to keep his distance.

"Do you have any brothers and sisters?" Michael asked as they approached Aaron's neighborhood.

"Nope, just me."

"Pets?"

Aaron laughed. "Yeah, like Tom would ever let me have a pet."

"I take it Tom's your stepdad," Michael said.

"Unfortunately," Aaron said, sorry for the reminder. "How 'bout you? Any family?"

Michael paused. Leafing through those memories was difficult for him – talking about it only served to make it real again. But it was he who had brought up the subject and he felt obliged to follow through.

"My wife and only son were killed in an auto accident," he said. The horrible memory flooded his senses.

"Oh, wow ..." Aaron said, unprepared for such a dismal reply. But he was able to relate – at least to some degree. "I'm so sorry."

"Thank you," Michael said. He hadn't spoken to anyone about it in years, and he felt the need to elaborate. "I wasn't with them that night. The other driver was drunk – he crossed over the center divide. Little Tyler was three; he was killed instantly. Jennie lived for 4 days." He paused for a moment to let his breath catch up. "It's been five-and-a-half years, now."

Aaron couldn't say anything, so he didn't try.

The Aston purred to a stop in front of Aaron's apartment. Aaron and Michael got out and walked up the front steps.

Michael removed a pad and pen from the inside pocket of his jacket, then scribbled something and tore out the page. "Here's my cell number," he said. "Call me tomorrow and let me know you're all right, okay?"

"Okay," Aaron said as he took the slip of paper.

Michael jotted down Aaron's number as well then raised a high-five. "You cool?" he asked.

Aaron fived him back. "Yeah, I'm cool. Thanks for the brownies."

He removed a key from under the welcome mat, unlocked the door, and replaced the key, then stepped inside and closed the heavy door behind him.

Michael laid his hand on the door and felt the grain of the wood.

"Good night, Aaron," he said.

As Michael drove away, he passed the white van, parked across the street from Aaron's apartment.

Johnny Souther was six blocks away, cruising the streets in a black van. He picked up Needles's call and listened for a moment.

"Hold your position," he said. "I'm on my way."

Chapter 14

BATTING PRACTICE

Aaron undressed, throwing his tattered clothes in the bottom of his hamper and covering them, making a mental note to trash them in the morning. He reached for his pajamas, but thinking again he decided to remain dressed. He put on a fresh pair of jeans, a T-shirt, a clean hooded sweatshirt, socks and sneakers.

He thought of waking his mother, but he couldn't face the prospect of waking Tom. So he crawled under the covers to wait for morning.

The black van pulled up to the apartment and parked behind the white van. Johnny Souther got out and walked over to meet with his thugs. Needles filled him in then told him about the hidden key.

"Guard the exits," Souther said as he reloaded his .45. "I'll take care of the kid. Stay outside even if shots are fired, understand? No one gets in or out alive." He pulled out a large knife and checked the edge with his thumb.

The thugs nodded, and Souther motioned for them to move out. He used the hidden key to unlock the front door, then drew his gun and quietly entered the apartment.

Aaron was wide awake when his bedroom door slowly

opened and the silhouette of a large man loomed in the doorway. He shuddered then watched in horror as the man picked up his little-league bat and slapped it repeatedly into his palm. *Smack ... Smack ... Smack ...*

"Out for a joy ride tonight, Aaron?" the man said.

Aaron was only partially relieved to recognize Tom's voice.

Suddenly Tom stopped, interrupted by a sound that came from downstairs. "Stay here," he said, motioning with his hand.

Tom stepped out into the hall and moved quietly toward the stairs to investigate. It occurred to him to get the .22 caliber pistol he kept loaded and ready in his sock drawer, but the apartment was old, and at night, when it was quiet, it wasn't unusual to hear strange sounds. He gripped the bat with both hands and slowly descended the dark stairs.

Souther was ascending the same stairs from below.

They met halfway.

Tom cried out and swung wildly. He heard a sickening thud, and the bat torqued in his hands as he connected with the side of Souther's head. Souther tumbled backward down the steps and lay motionless at the bottom of the dark stairwell. Tom's heart pounded the breath from his lungs.

Ashley hadn't slept since Aaron ran away, and when she heard the fighting she grabbed her eyeglasses off the night table, jumped out of bed, and threw on her poly satin robe. She hesitated, then ran to Tom's dresser and retrieved his .22, a compact yet lethal weapon of which she had always disapproved. Then she clicked on the hall light and ran to the top of the stairs.

She saw her husband, Aaron's baseball bat, and the

shadowed stranger sprawled across the bottom steps.

"*Thomas?*" she cried.

Tom looked up and saw her holding the gun.

"Shoot the bastard!" he shouted.

"*What?* I –"

"Kill the son-of-a-bitch!"

Ashley pointed the gun at Souther, but hesitated.

Souther came to and scrabbled around for his pistol.

"Oh, God!" Tom cried. "Shoot him, Ashley! *Kill him!*"

Ashley closed her eyes, fired and missed – the feel of the lethal round exiting the barrel sickened her.

Souther found his gun, whipped it up and fired. The bullet smacked Tom in the chest, slamming him against the wall and sending the bat flying.

Ashley screamed, fired again, and missed. Souther looked up at her, and for an instant their eyes met. Then she ran back upstairs, knowing her husband was dead.

Souther stood and started up the stairs after her. Tom was sprawled on the steps, blood soaking into the carpet beneath him. Souther heard him groan, so he shot him again. Then he stepped over the body and continued up the stairs, reloading as he went.

Ashley ran into her son at the top of the stairs. He had seen everything.

"Aaron!" she cried, surprised, delighted, and terrified to discover that he had returned home.

"Follow me," he said, snatching some car keys, a credit card, and a cell phone from the hall table. They ducked into his bedroom and he dead-bolted the door behind them.

He slid the window open and climbed out onto the flat roof

over the garage. "Give me your hand," he said, holding out his. "Hurry!" Ashley took his hand and stepped quickly through the window onto sharp gravel that cut into her bare feet.

Aaron lead the way across the rooftop to the fire ladder, then motioned for her to wait as he peered over the edge of the low parapet. In the dark alley below he saw the huge black man from the cannery standing guard a few feet from the bottom of the ladder – he had his gun in his hand.

Ashley shivered in her thin robe and nightgown. "I-I let Tom d-die tonight," she said.

"What? No you didn't."

"I c-couldn't shoot."

Aaron huddled closer to her, not knowing what to say. He was struggling with his own feelings regarding Tom's death. He noticed the bruise under her eye, and he didn't have to ask her how she got it.

He refocused his attention on his plan. "Mom, listen to me," he said. "We're going to use the fire escape and make a run for the garage. I'll go first ... then I'll help you, okay?"

Ashley looked at him, clutching the neck of her nightgown. The plan terrified her.

Aaron sensed her trepidation. "We have no other choice," he said. "If we don't move fast they'll find us and kill us." He placed the keys, credit card, and phone in her hands and squeezed them. "Take these ... you've got bigger pockets than I do." The pockets in his jeans were fine, of course, but in the likelihood that he and his mother got separated during the escape, he figured she could use them more than he.

He remembered that she had had Tom's gun, and for a brief insane moment he thought they might be able to shoot their way out.

"Do you still have the gun?" he asked.

Ashley felt the cold steel pressing against her thigh and she nodded. But as she went to pull the .22 out of the pocket of her robe, Aaron came to his senses and laid his hand on her arm. His gun handling skills, although excellent, were limited to video games. He wouldn't stand a chance in a real gunfight, against what was likely a highly trained professional killer. Besides, if they did get separated, he'd want her to have the pistol as well.

"No," he said. "You keep it."

"Really? But you –"

Aaron squeezed her arm, nearly to the point of hurting her.

"Keep it," he said.

Ashley looked at her son for a moment, struggling with her thoughts. Everything was happening too fast. Then she let the gun slide back into its satin holster.

Aaron looked at her squarely. "No police ... okay, Mom?"

"What?"

"Trust me," he said. "You don't want to call the cops on these guys. Not yet, at least."

Ashley had never seen Aaron act this way before – like a man – and she felt the warmth of maternal pride move through her. It relaxed her a little and quelled some of her fear. But still she struggled to hold back her tears.

Aaron stood and breathed deeply. What they were about to attempt terrified him, too. "Okay, then ..." he said. "Let's do this."

Chapter 15

300 Horses

Blood streamed down the side of Souther's face as he checked the upstairs of the apartment. In the master bath he found a clean towel and used it to wipe his face. Then he pressed it against his scalp to control the bleeding. He saw a utility bill lying on the dresser: It was addressed to an Ashley Quinn. He noted the name and left the room.

He crossed the hall and tried Aaron's door, but it was bolted. He slammed his shoulder into it, but the door held.

Again.

The door held.

He fired a bullet into the lock, but the lock held.

"Shit!" he said, enraged. Then he headed back downstairs.

Aaron peered over the edge of the roof and down into the dark alley. The gunman was still only a few yards away. Aaron knew that the last section of the rickety fire ladder was missing, leaving an eight-foot drop to the pavement. This wasn't going to be easy.

He steeled himself then climbed over the edge and down the ladder where he hung from the last corroded rung for a moment before dropping to the street. He crouched low against the wall, watching the gunman, then looked up and gestured to his mother to follow him.

Ashley edged herself out over the parapet and onto the iron ladder, her hands trembling uncontrollably as her body tried to ward off hypothermia.

"Hey!" a voice boomed, sending a cold thrill of terror lancing up Aaron's back. Ashley leaped back onto the roof, stifling a cry as the sharp stones cut into her feet.

Aaron turned to run, but as he did an immense, powerful hand landed heavily on his shoulder and in an instant the hard black asphalt rushed up and smashed into him like a bus. He gasped for breath, crying out silently to his mother, *Run when you can, Mom! Run to the Nova!* But all he could do was grit his teeth in pain and prepare to meet his fate.

Ashley peeked over the edge and watched helplessly as Beeks dragged Aaron down the alley and around the corner of the building. She was nearly hysterical, her face awash with tears, her mind spinning out wild imaginings of what they would do to him. But she knew what she had to do if she was ever going to see him again. So she calmed herself, said a short prayer, and set her mind on escaping.

Though still fit and agile at thirty-four, she had difficulty with the final drop to the street, hitting the pavement hard, twisting her bare ankle sharply. She grimaced in pain, then braced one hand against the rough stucco wall, with the other under her torn ankle, and hopped over to the small door into the garage.

Johnny Souther caught up with Needles in the side alley. "I think they went out the back," he said, looking up at the roof over the garage. "Where's Beeks?"

"He was guarding the rear," Needles said. He noticed the

fresh blood on Souther's face. "I heard shots. Are you okay?"

Souther started toward the back alley. "Let's just say I stood too close during batting practice, and the batter had to be taken out of the game."

Just then Beeks showed up dragging his prize along side him. Souther saw Aaron and seized him violently from behind and thrust his knife up under his chin, nearly breaking Aaron's arm with his powerful hold.

"You cost me a lot of time and trouble tonight, punk," Souther said, teeth clenched. He tightened his grip with a grunt. "Now it's payback time."

Aaron was consumed by fear, unable to think or move as the cold sharp blade quivered beneath his jaw. But just as Souther went to slit Aaron's throat he stopped and looked at Beeks.

"Where's the woman?" he said.

Beeks was still patting himself on the back for rounding up the boy. "Woman?" he said, surprised by the question.

"The kid's mother, damn it!" Souther said. "The lady whose husband I just killed. She can ID me, for Christ's sake." He glanced up toward the roof again.

Behind the wheel of the Nova, now, Ashley fumbled desperately with the keys.

Beeks was sure that the boy had been alone. "I never seen any –"

"Shut up ..." Souther said, cutting Beeks off at the sound of a car starting. He tossed Aaron to Needles and ran toward the garage, yelling over his shoulder: "Take care of the kid ... we may need him."

Ashley gripped the wheel and mashed the Nova's

accelerator through the floorboards. The small-block V-8 coughed twice, then responded with a throaty glass-pack roar, sending all 300 screaming horses to wide rear tires that billowed thick white smoke like a coal-fired locomotive.

The little Chevy smashed through the wooden garage door in a shower of splinters, narrowly missing Johnny Souther before swerving off down the alley and out of sight.

Neighborhood dogs barked hysterically as Souther slowly picked himself up off the pavement.

Chapter 16

THE PHOTO

The two vans pulled inside the cannery, and everyone got out. Beeks rolled the big door closed, and Needles lit a gasoline lantern.

"Put him over there and tie him up," Souther said, pointing to a chair in a corner.

Beeks led Aaron to the chair and as he turned to grab a roll of duct tape to secure him, Aaron quickly slipped Michael's cell number into his shoe.

Souther walked over and went through Aaron's pockets.

"Did you call the cops?" Souther asked.

Aaron still struggled with his decision not to. "No," he replied.

"Good. Because you'd have signed your mother's death warrant."

Souther found Aaron's wallet and inside it a small snapshot. He held the photo up to the lamplight. It was the shot of Aaron's mother and father in the alpine meadow. There were very few photos taken of his parents together and to Aaron this one was priceless.

"Give me that!" he cried, straining against his bindings. "That's mine!"

Souther had gotten a brief look at the boy's mother back at the apartment, but it had been dark, and he could see that she was much more beautiful – and desirable – than he remembered.

"I can see where you get your good looks, kid," he said. "How old's the photo?"

"I don't know," Aaron said stubbornly. "I want it back."

Souther turned away and studied the photo. Ashley's large eyes looked straight into the lens, her lithe body was turned slightly toward the camera as she leaned into her man, her slender arms around his neck, a breast pressed lightly against his powerful bicep, a bare foot raised a few inches off the grass, her shorts and halter top seemingly airbrushed on. Souther felt a stirring in his loins as he took it all in.

"We'd better get moving," Needles said.

Souther took a moment to archive the delicious image ... then he tossed the photo to Needles. Needles stared at Ashley for a long moment. Beeks took a look for himself over Needles's shoulder.

"Her name's Ashley Quinn," Souther said, using the name from the electric bill. "You know what to do ..."

"We'll find her," Needles said.

"On your way out, drop by the apartment and clean up the mess on the stairs," Souther said.

"Will do," Needles said. He pocketed the photo then climbed into the white van and fired up the engine. Beeks opened the large roll-up door, then jumped in with him.

Souther called to Needles. "Don't lose that picture ... I want it back."

Needles smiled to himself, thinking, *Like that would ever happen.*

Then the two thugs headed out into the city.

Chapter 17

COLD CONCRETE

Souther rolled the big door closed, then walked over and cut Aaron's restraints. He picked up the lamp and led Aaron to the cannery's main floor break room: a space the size of large bedroom with a kitchenette; a legless, maroon-velvet sofa; and a large, heavy wooden table.

There was a small door in the back of the room that Aaron and Willy had always been too afraid to open. Souther didn't have that problem, of course. Without hesitation he turned the knob and opened the door wide.

A clammy vapor wafted up into Aaron's face, smelling of mold and urine. It was icy cold and damp against his skin, contradicting the Biblical fire-and-brimstone he had expected to encounter in hell.

"Go on down," Souther said, gesturing with the lantern.

Aaron could only imagine the myriad of horrors waiting for him down those stairs. He stepped cautiously through the low door and started down the steep steps. Souther followed closely, his lantern casting a hazy gloom over the forbidding space as they descended into thickening darkness.

At last Aaron's shoes found the packed earth of a dirt floor, and he paused to look around. The room was basically a rough concrete cube, about ten by ten feet, and mostly empty.

Souther set the lantern on a box and pointed to a corner.

"There's a coffee can over there if you need to pee," he said. "When you're ready to talk, bang on the door and someone will hear you." Then he turned and climbed back up the stairs.

Aaron sat down heavily on a blue plastic milk crate. There was a fresh bottle of water sitting in the dirt next to him. He looked at it for a moment. *They say you can last three weeks without food*, he thought, *but only three days without water.* Then he twisted it open and drank deeply.

Souther paused near the top of the stairs. "I'll find your mother with or without your help, kid," he said. Then he ducked through the door and locked it behind him.

Aaron screwed the cap back onto the bottle and set it in on the box with the lantern. Then he leaned back against the cold concrete wall and fell asleep.

Chapter 18

THE BOILER HOUSE

Needles and Beeks were in the white van heading back to the cannery. They had succeeded in cleaning up the apartment and had Tom's body stashed in the back of the van.

Beeks rode shotgun. "I'm hungry," he announced.

"You're kidding me," Needles said. "Fifteen minutes ago I watched you down five beef n' cheese burritos, two sides of beans, and a boatload of chips."

Beeks thought about that for a moment. "I only had one thing of beans," he said, "and them burritos was plain – no fuckin' cheese."

"How would you know? The whole meal only lasted thirty seconds."

"Yeah ... well, I know one thing, motherfucker, you're wrong about what I ate, and I'm fuckin' hungry."

"That's two things, dumbass. And I'm never wrong."

"The hell you ain't."

Needles paused, then said thoughtfully, "Yeah, well, I thought I was wrong once ... but it turned out I was right. So, I guess I was wrong about that."

"Fuck you."

"Well, I'm not stopping again."

"I'm starving, and you could give a shit," Beeks said.

"Doesn't your wife ever feed you?"

"No."

"So why'd you marry her?"

"Does your wife feed you?"

"She would if I had one."

"Kiss my ass."

Johnny Souther hated to be cold, an obsession he picked up after many chilly years in Northern prisons, and his men were instructed to keep the cannery furnace firing full blast. The heat came from radiators supplied by steam from a natural-gas-fired boiler, as the city had neglected to shut off the gas when condemning the building. The current boiler, housed in a brick-and-mortar boiler house attached to the rear of the cannery in the area of the shipping yard, was installed as part of the 1907 reconstruction following the accident that destroyed it in 1905.

Needles and Beeks entered the boiler house struggling with the dead-weight of their load. Beeks had the shoulders and Needles the feet.

"I got the heavy fuckin' half," Beeks grunted.

"Like hell you did," Needles said, gritting his teeth.

The huge welded-steel replacement boiler (converted from coal to gas in 1965), was 17 feet long and six feet in diameter and nearly filled the space. Years of greasy soot clung to every surface and caulked every crevice. Shafts of firelight flashed through the boiler-oven's vent slots, generating brilliant patterns on the blackened brick walls.

The thugs dropped the body in front of the furnace, creating plumes of ash. Beeks yanked on the lever and when he pulled the massive cast-iron door open a blast of super-heated air knocked them both back a step.

"Son-of-a-bitch!" Beeks exclaimed, feeling his forehead. "I think I'm missing a damn eyebrow."

"As if you had any to begin with," Needles said.

"Bite me," Beeks said.

They hefted the body again and shuffled up to the brink of the inferno.

"Let's get it right this time," Needles said, turning his face away from the heat of the flames. "I don't want a repeat of the last horror show."

Beeks nodded – he remembered it well. They had muffed the toss and the corpse had landed half in and half out of the roaring furnace; and by the time they managed to stuff the rest of the body inside and shut the door, the sight and smell of it had nearly killed them both.

Needles called the count: "On three, ready? One ... two ... *heave!*"

Chapter 19

SUN-DRIED SQUID

The thugs showed Ashley's picture to everyone they met: shop owners, passers by, vagrants, motel clerks.

The trail led them to an all-night gas station located out on the old highway, west of town. Needles pulled off onto the muddy drive, then rolled the van's front tires up against a railroad tie and killed the engine.

Beeks thought they'd arrived in the Old West: the hitching rails; the wagon wheels; the ancient, glass-top fuel pump out front. Needles marveled that the property was wired for electricity.

They glanced at each other then stepped out of the van and started toward the office.

Out of nowhere, a tall, shirtless, ninety-year-old strip of beef jerky wrapped in denim coveralls, a straw cowboy hat, and ancient snakeskin boots appeared. His faded, pink-paisley neckerchief looked like a rope quoit tossed over a stake. Beeks took a half step back, convinced that they had traveled back in time.

The old man was visibly grateful for the company, speaking in an aristocratic, yet lively manner that belied his years.

"Greetings, friends," he said nobly, his s's making short whistling sounds as they passed through the gap where his front teeth used to be. "To what do I owe the honor of your visit?"

"Greetings to you, sir," Needles replied, then asked him if he'd mind answering some questions. The old man nodded and invited them inside.

The business office was little more than a shack; however, a couple of years back, in a sad effort that consumed the bulk of the old man's life savings, he had converted it into a miniature convenience store complete with wall-length cooler, credit-card reader, and surveillance camera.

The card reader actually functioned, but the camera was a cardboard fake, and most of the food in the cooler was stocked there when the unit was originally installed. Beeks grabbed a pre-packaged ham 'n cheddar sandwich from the cooler, but he changed his mind about eating it when he noticed some extra protein running around under the cellophane and a sell-by date from the Great Depression.

An open bottle of premium whiskey stood on the counter by the register near a baby-moon hubcap full of cigarette butts – one of which was still smoldering. The old man picked up the bottle and turned to his guests.

"Would you boys care to join me?" he asked.

"Sure, old man," Needles said. "We'll drink with you." His answer surprised Beeks, since they were "on duty," but he wasn't about to argue.

The old man poured, and the three men clinked glasses before downing the shots. Beeks smacked his sizable lips and burped, then shoved his glass forward for seconds.

Needles took out Ashley's photo and showed it to the old man. He studied it at arm's length for a while, and judging by his reaction, his eyesight and hormones were still functioning reasonably well.

"She was here, all right," he said at last. "I remember, 'cause I used to have a '65 just like hers – 'cept mine had a stick instead'a the Powerglide. I topped her off, and she bought grape juice, crackers, and a pint of gin."

Beeks doubted the wisdom of the non-alcoholic portion of that purchase.

The old man continued. "I figured she was some sort of outa-town movie star or somethin' – bein' so uncommonly pretty and drivin' around town in her negligee and all. But she was acting strange – kinda nervous I guess you'd say. And she had this look in her eye – like someone barely clinging to sanity."

Needles thought about that for a moment, then laid a $50 bill on the counter.

The old man's silver-thatched eyebrows twitched at the sight of it – it had been a long time since he'd seen anything larger than a $5. He pulled a wadded, white-lace-bordered handkerchief out of his pocket, put it to his lips, and coughed something disgusting into it. The thugs tried not to imagine what it was, but they couldn't help themselves.

"Which way did she go?" Needles asked, swallowing involuntarily.

"I'd say west," the old man replied confidently. He pointed in that direction like a roasted chicken stretching its wing. "I could hardly believe her little Chevy was still a runnin', with its front-end smashed in so. But it weren't leakin' and one of her headlights was lit ... so I let her be." He coughed more of the mystery substance into his handkerchief. "One damn-crazy customer – that's what she was."

"Thanks, old man," Needles said, shoving the $50 forward. He shook the man's hand, taking care not to crack it. *Like squeezing a sun-dried squid*, he thought.

The old man nodded and tipped his hat. Then Needles and Beeks headed back outside and continued down the highway.

Chapter 20

THE CALL

Ashley watched as raindrops began to hit random targets on her windshield. They developed into a downpour and her wipers were of little effect as she strained to see the road through the chaotic blackness. She was headed west out the old highway with no idea where she was going. All she could think to do was to run, so running she was.

She had the heater in the old Chevy cranked on high, but still she shivered, unable to shake the horrible feeling that she had abandoned her only son to a pack of hungry wolves.

But what could she have done? Call out from the top of the fire ladder? *I'm here! Come get me, I'm here!* She was free to help Aaron, now, and that was a good thing – at least that's what she kept telling herself.

But she had no clue where to begin. Tom's murder was nothing more than a burglary that had gone horribly wrong. She had no idea that the gunman had intended to kill Aaron.

She glanced at the cell phone lying on the seat next to her and recalled that special moment when Aaron had given it to her. How strong and courageous he had been. How grown up. She questioned her decision to follow his orders not to call the police, and wondered if she would ever see him again.

Suddenly an idea occurred to her that might have seemed obvious under normal circumstances. She picked up the phone, took a deep breath, and called her son.

Souther was alone in his office when Aaron's cell phone rang. He saw the word MOM displayed on the screen.

"Hello, Ashley," he said, in a cruelly relaxed voice. "My name is Johnny Souther. I have your son."

"*Oh my God ...*" she thought, a sharp pang of horror sweeping through her. She swerved hard left to avoid sliding off the dark highway.

"Listen carefully," Souther said.

"Where's Aaron? I want to see my son."

"Aaron is unharmed."

Ashley closed her eyes and thanked God for small miracles.

"I want you to listen for a moment," Souther said. "Can you do that?"

Ashley gripped the steering wheel tightly and tried to collect herself. This man had just gunned down her husband in cold blood and he was no doubt planning a similar fate for her and her son.

"Your son's in a safe place," Souther said, "and he'll remain safe as long as you do exactly as I say. Do you understand?""

Ashley began to weep. "Yes," she said.

"Did you call the police?"

No."

"Good," Souther said. "Let's keep it that way. If you call the cops, your son's dead."

Ashley took in a quick breath. That was the first time she'd heard those dreaded words spoken out loud.

"Do you have money for a motel?" Souther said.

Ashley paused, then replied, "Yes."

"Okay. I want you to get a room and stay there. Do you understand?"

She wanted to ask, *Why the room? Why not take me now?*

but didn't. "I understand," she said.

"I have some business to attend to," Souther said. "Your son will be safe until I return – unless, of course, someone does something stupid while I'm gone. I'll contact you with further instructions."

"What do you *want* from us?" Ashley cried. But the call was dead.

Needles's phone rang, and he picked up.

"I just got a call from Ashley Quinn," Souther said.

"Oh, really ..." Needles said, surprised, but interested.

"Any leads?"

"Someone saw her out on the old highway," Needles said. "We'll have her soon enough."

"Good," Souther said, "but swing by my office first. I want to have a little fun with her."

Needles hung up and set his phone aside. He wasn't sure what Souther meant by that (and it was a long drive back to the cannery), but having fun with a beautiful woman always sounded good to him – and orders were orders.

"Hold on, Beeks," he said. Then he reached for the hand brake and to the big man's dismay, pulled a violent E-brake U-turn in the middle of the highway and headed the van back toward the city, leaving a curling wake of white smoke trailing behind them.

Chapter 21

SANDS MOTEL

Emerging from the gloom, beyond the reach of her headlights, Ashley could see a large, brightly lit sign in the shape of a palm tree. As she drew nearer she was able to make out the words SANDS MOTEL, and soon the word VACANCY floated into view. She eased off the gas, crossed over the centerline, and pulled into the narrow driveway – gripping the steering wheel tightly as her Chevy rocked and splashed through pothole craters blown out of the asphalt by the parade of eighteen-wheelers from the motel's glory days.

She had hoped for something a little nicer than a moribund hovel, but this was the first sign of life since the old man's gas station several miles back, and being unfamiliar with the area, she wasn't certain there *were* any other motels – or that she could afford a better one if she found one. Besides, the lights were on and she was too exhausted to drive.

The motel was a squat, flat-roofed, lagoon-green and tangerine affair with little palm trees cut out of fake window shutters. Ashley guessed that the owners were going for the Florida Keys look, but had failed miserably.

The office sat to the right of a lattice-covered breezeway furnished with a half-dozen plastic lounge chairs and a ping-pong table that sagged pathetically under its own waterlogged weight. Jutting off to the left, a wing of seven small guest rooms, each with its false-louver door flaking a different color of paint from a pastel palette. Ashley parked the car, shut off the engine, and stepped out into the weather.

The rain-charged wind cut through her paper-thin robe and nightgown as though she were naked. She clutched her robe to her throat and hopped quickly toward the glowing OFFICE sign, pausing briefly under the covered porch to look back across the parking lot and down the old highway beyond. Then she opened the door and stepped inside.

The office interior looked like a nineteenth-century séance parlor, and along with the tasseled draperies and woven rugs, Ashley half expected to see a crystal ball, or a flying trumpet, or maybe a rattling tambourine circling the naked light bulb jutting from the dark wooden ceiling. She wrinkled her nose at the strong odor of wet dog and presumed that the source of the smell was curled up behind the tattered royal-blue-velvet curtain hanging behind the counter.

It was quiet in the parlor. Ashley's head throbbed as if someone had grabbed her heart and shoved it up behind her eyes. She banged the push bell and thought she'd been caught in a cathedral belfry at noon bells.

She waited, but no one came. So she pressed her fingers against her temples and called out. "Hello? Is anyone there?"

Nothing.

She braced herself and tried the push bell again.

More pain, but still no response.

A clock on the mantelpiece read 11:45 p.m. Ashley sighed, and then cold, wet, exhausted (and now annoyed), she turned to leave.

Suddenly, from behind her, a voice croaked, "May I help you?"

Ashley whirled around with a hand over her heart. An odd little man appeared from behind the blue curtain looking like he'd been awakened from a five-year coma. His print pajamas and tousled comb-over fit the decor, as if he had used them for design ideas when he decorated the place a couple of centuries earlier.

Ashley paused to recover her breath. "You scared me," she said.

A light cloud of dust from the curtain followed the man as he stepped up to the counter, and Ashley noticed that his chin barely cleared the Formica top. He squinted in the light and picked small clumps of sleep from the corners of his puffy eyes.

"May I help you?" he repeated, then yawned deeply and rubbed his stubby nose with his thumb.

"Uh, yes – hello," Ashley said, with nervous formality. "I-I'd like a room please. Do you have a vacancy?" She could only see the man's head, now, but she could smell the rest of him. *That was no dog behind the curtain*, she thought, stepping back slightly.

Out of habit the little man checked the board. Each brass cup-hook held its key. He coughed once to clear his throat.

"I've got an available single," he said, then looked back at her. "If that'll do, that is ..."

"It will do," Ashley replied, feeling a pinch of relief. She pictured a clean room and fresh sheets and started to relax. "I don't know how long I'll be –"

"It don't matter," the man said, interrupting her as he pushed the registration book forward. "It's pay as you leave." He pointed to a line on the page. "Sign here."

Ashley picked up the pen then hesitated. She signed the

name *Arlene Finney* then laid the pen on the book and pushed it back.

The little man read her entry. "Arleeene ..." he said, stretching out the second syllable for no apparent reason before putting out his hand. "My name's Mars – Douglas Mars. Friends call me Doolin."

What friends? Ashley wondered, finding it hard to imagine him having any. She reluctantly shook Doolin's pudgy hand then wiped hers on her robe while trying not to make a face. *Like gripping a warm toad*, she thought, disgusted.

"You from around here ... Arlene?" Doolin asked, pronouncing her pseudonym correctly, now – if not a bit suspiciously.

Ashley felt a growing unease. "Actually, I'm from – out of town." She had started to say, *I'm from another planet*, for that's certainly how she felt.

"We don't get many visitors these days," Doolin said. "Not since the freeway bypass, anyways."

Ashley hadn't heard that old cliché in years and never outside of a movie theater. But thinking about it made her head hurt and she grew impatient. "Could I just have my key, please?"

Doolin held up his hands in self-defense. "Just tryin' to be neighborly," he said. He turned and unhooked a key from the board, then tossed it on the counter. "Room 107. It's on the end past the ice machine. Nice and private."

Private from whom? Ashley wondered as she stared at the key and began to have serious second thoughts.

"I think maybe – uh ..." She paused, then told herself, *You're here, okay? Stop being a baby and make the best of it.* The quality of her lodging *was*, after all, the least of her worries.

"Room 107 will be fine," she said at last. She picked up the key then paused. "You wouldn't happen to have a vending machine, or somewhere I can get something to eat, would you?"

"Sorry," Doolin replied. "There's a coffee shop a few miles –"

"Oh, I don't – I mean, I'd rather stay in tonight," Ashley said, reminding herself not to let her stomach speak for her in the future. She turned and started out the door.

"By chance is there somebody lookin' for you, Miss Arlene?" Doolin asked, his voice taking on the air of a small-town deputy sheriff.

Ashley stopped, shocked by the question, and turned to face him. "No, of course not," she replied, trying to maintain a casual confidence in her voice. "W-why would you ask such a thing?"

Doolin stared at Ashley's bruised eye; then his eyes moved slowly down over her perfect body. "Oh, I don't know," he said. "You just seem a little ... *tight*."

Ashley's eyes followed Doolin's and she nearly screamed when she saw that her rain-soaked nightwear had become see-through, and that the cold had had its stimulating effect. She stepped back in horror and crossed her arms over her breasts.

"I have to go," she said, face flushed. Then she turned and hurried out the door.

"Ring the bell if you need anything," Doolin said after her. "Just ring the bell ..."

He copped a last look before Ashley slammed the door behind her. Then he closed the registration book and smiled.

Chapter 22

ROOM 107

Rain continued to fall as Ashley limped painfully across the empty parking lot to her Chevy. She looked around then opened the car door and climbed into the driver's seat.

She shut the door and sat for a while with her hands resting on the wheel. Rain drummed the roof and splashed the glass as she peered out at a distorted image of the Sands Motel.

She thought of Danny and of their wedding day, of how handsome he had been in his dress uniform. So tall and strong. So desirable. She remembered how hard it had rained at his funeral, and how the American flag draped over the casket had gotten wet, and how she'd been concerned after hearing of an incident where a wet lowering strap had snapped, allowing the coffin to fall into the grave where the lid broke loose and exposed the body to the entire assembly.

She gripped the wheel tightly, fighting the urge to scream, then shook the disturbing image out of her mind.

You can drive away, she thought desperately. *You can start the damn car and drive away.*

Go ahead, Ashley, a second voice countered, *drive on out of here. But don't say I didn't warn you when you fall asleep at the wheel and kill yourself.*

She reached across the seat and grabbed the two shopping

bags and stepped out of the car into the rain again. Then she hobbled the short distance to Room 107.

The first to assault Ashley's senses, the eye-watering odor – as if someone had dumped a truckload of rotting cabbage in the room and sealed it shut for ten years. She switched to mouth breathing and wished she had purchased some surgeon's gloves back at the drug store.

All around her, flower patterned wallpaper blistered and peeled from the crumbling plaster like a severe case of motel eczema. Discolored carpeting in front of the TV betrayed the likely truth that something had died there in recent months. Jammed against one wall, a small bed, its lumpy spread a montage of stains. Above it, an oil-on-black-velvet matador, its fuzzy texture (and most of the sequins adorning the cape) long since rubbed off. From a shelf, a dusty oscillating fan wheezed back and forth, ruffling her wet hair in a vain attempt to cool the air, its gear-drive skipping and jumping, each erratic sweep of the room likely to be its last.

She flopped the large plastic shopping bag on the bed; then from the smaller bag, she removed a half-full quart of grape juice, a half-eaten box of crackers, and a pint of gin, and set them on the night table along with her car keys, credit card and phone. She dumped the contents of the other bag out onto the bed: a lavender faux-suede jacket; a sundress; a white bra and three pairs of panties; a men's white undershirt and pair of boxer shorts (make-shift pajamas, like the ones she used to borrow from Danny); miscellaneous toiletries, pills, and makeup accessories; a simple necklace; and a pair of low heels. She draped the jacket over a chair and smoothed the wrinkles out of the new sundress.

She walked over to a vanity mirror with half of its silvered glass falling from the frame, and as she ran a brush through her hair she regarded a strange reflection with its Picassoesque interpretation of her tired eyes. The bruise under her right eye was getting darker, and she cringed at that frightening memory.

She smoothed her cheeks with her hands and sighed. Her youth was slipping away – falling through her fingers like a handful of rose petals. *I'll continue to feel young*, she thought. *I know I will. I always have. But one day the world will take a vote and decide that I'm old.* But tonight she didn't feel young at all. Tonight she felt very old.

She tore the price tag off of a new vinyl purse and stowed the brush inside. Then she opened a bottle of acetaminophen 500s, removed the cotton padding, shook three capsules into the palm of her hand, and downed them with a swallow of grape juice. She capped the bottle and tossed it in the purse, then went over and shoved the handgun between the mattresses.

Just then the white van pulled up and parked near the Sands Motel office. The thugs got out and went inside.

Doolin stared at Ashley's picture, tracing the lines of her body with his eyes and imagining himself there in her arms. He would have sold his soul for a copy. "Oh, I'd remember her," he said, picturing Ashley as she walked out the door in her see-through nightwear. "But the truth is, we don't get a lot of visitors out here these days – not since the freeway bypass anyways."

The thugs looked at each other. There was no freeway

bypass.

Needles laid a $50 on the counter. "Take a closer look," he said. "She's four or five years older, now."

Doolin scooped up the money and clutched it tightly in his fist. Then he took another long look at the photo. "Like I said ... I never seen –"

Beeks snatched the $50, and with one powerful hand he grabbed Doolin by his pajama collar and lifted him off his feet. "You're a lying sack-of-shit," he said, his huge face within inches of Doolin's.

Doolin couldn't make a sound. Blood backed up in his veins like a web of tiny stopped-up sewer drains, turning his complexion three shades darker than its usual alcohol-induced rouge.

Needles noticed only one key missing from its hook on the board – number 107. "Put him down, Beeks," he said calmly.

Beeks gave Needles a puzzled look and held Doolin even higher. "What'd you say?"

"I said 'Let the man go.'"

"Brother, I don't get you sometimes," Beeks said, shaking his head. He gave Doolin a toss that sent him sprawling.

Doolin gasped and wheezed and then climbed to his feet and held onto the counter while the excess blood drained from his head. He looked at Needles through watering eyes and straightened his pajama collar. "Ahem," he coughed. "As I was –"

"Shut up, asshole," Needles said, "and thank the good Lord you're still breathing." He slipped Ashley's picture back into his pocket and glanced at Beeks. "Let's go," he said, and they turned and walked out.

Ashley pulled back the shower curtain, turned on the water, and adjusted the cracked-porcelain knobs until she arrived at a comfortable temperature. Then she dropped her filthy robe and slipped out of her tattered nightgown and stepped into the tub. She flipped the water flow to the shower head and stood for a while, watching the water circle the drain, letting the soothing warmth flow over her neck and shoulders. She poured a generous dab of body wash into her hand and slowly lathered her aching body. Then she turned up the hot water and as the bathroom fill with steam, she began to cry.

The rain had eased a bit outside Room 107, and the thugs could hear the shower running. Beeks deftly picked the lock then opened the door slightly. Needles used bolt-cutters to dispatch the security chain, and then he and Beeks stepped inside.

Beeks watched the bathroom door while Needles removed something from his pocket and laid it on Ashley's pillow; then the two thugs stepped outside and quietly closed the door.

Chapter 23

SANDWICHES

Ashley returned from her shower wrapped in a towel. She sat on the edge of the bed and contemplated the bottle of gin sitting on the night table. She picked it up and unscrewed the cap, but as she raised it to her lips she hesitated.

What the hell are you doing? she thought, disgusted with herself. *What possible good will getting shit-faced do? You're not a drinker! Aaron needs you sober, you stupid cow!*

She stepped into the bathroom and poured the gin down the toilet.

There was a loud knock that sent a chill down her spine. She set the empty gin bottle on the sink, retrieved the .22 from between the mattresses, and stepped cautiously over to peer through the peep-hole. A grotesque fish-eye image of Doolin Mars stared up at her; he appeared to be carrying a tray. She raised her pistol and took a deep breath; then, failing to notice that the security chain had been cut, she opened the door a crack.

Doolin had dressed for the occasion (if a lime-green sweatsuit could be considered dressed). He held up the tray and said proudly, "I made sandwiches."

Ashley was struck speechless. She was starving, but she would eat the socks off an NFL lineman after a big game before she'd touch anything from Doolin's tray. "I – uh ... I-I'm not really hungry," she said.

"But you said –"

"I lost my appetite." She started to close the door, but Doolin jammed it with his foot.

"Some men came looking for you tonight, Arlene," he said, trying to get a look at her through the door.

Ashley froze. "What? When? What did you tell them?"

Doolin was surprised and hurt by the question. "Why, I didn't tell them nothin'," he said. "You should know your secret's safe with me, Miss Arlene." He withdrew his foot and looked up at her hopefully.

"Goodnight, Doolin," Ashley said. Then she closed the door and locked it.

As she leaned back against the door, she saw the cut security chain hanging limp next to her ear. "Oh my *God*," she cried. Then with the gun aimed at the peep-hole, she stepped back and sat down on the edge of the bed.

From the driver's seat in the white van, Needles could see Doolin in his green outfit scuttling back to the motel office. He made a call and Souther answered from his office.

"We have our girl," Needles said.

"Did you make the plant?"

"That's affirmative."

They ended the call, and Needles drove slowly out of the motel parking lot.

Ashley watched the door for several minutes. Then as she started to lie back on the bed she saw something on her pillow. She bolted upright, eyes wide, and stared at it for a moment, her hand to her throat. *Someone had been in her room!*

She tried to think rationally, fighting the urge to panic. She set the gun aside, and with trembling hands, picked up the small digital recorder and pressed PLAY.

Souther's recorded voice was tinny and distorted, but recognizable:

"Bravo for following my instructions, Ashley. You were smart not to call the police. Do us all a favor and stay where you are. I've taken care of things at your apartment, and I'll contact you when I'm ready."

Ashley shook the player, as if to coax more from it. "What about Aaron?" she cried. "I want to see my baby!" She shook the player again then heaved it at the wall where it shattered to pieces.

Chapter 24

APPLAUSE

Aaron held the gasoline lantern high, searching his basement cell for a way out, but the four concrete-block walls offered little encouragement. He climbed the stairs and tried the door. But as he expected, it was locked.

From the stair landing he had a different perspective on the space. He could see that the block walls only went about half way up – eight feet maybe – with wood-framing continuing the rest of the way to the joists high above. He noticed what appeared to be a small casement window on the far side of the room cut into the wood-framed portion of the wall about ten feet off the floor – it had been blacked out with spray paint. He felt a pang of hope as the window appeared to be reachable via a narrow ledge that ran along the tops of the concrete walls where the wood framing met the block. He set the lantern down on the landing and stepped out onto the precarious ledge.

He had to take care not to lose his footing, as every few inches a foundation bolt tried to trip him up, and a thick coating of gritty dust made the going even more treacherous. He used the exposed wooden 2x6 wall studs as handholds and dodged protruding nails that jabbed at his face and sticky cobwebs that tugged his hair.

He looked down, and he was higher than he thought – a fall from here would make the headlines. He continued on until at last he reached the small window, then flipped the latch and cranked it open.

The window opened outward at about three feet above ground level. The skies had cleared, and a cold wind blew through his hair and chilled his face as he stuck his head out to take a look. The moon was full, and he was able to see out across the ruins of the cannery's shipping yard.

The yard was a rectangular space about half a football field in area, bordered on two sides by the towering walls of the L-shaped cannery. The basement window where Aaron stood was beneath the east wing – the short leg of the L – that formed the eastern boundary of the yard; the main warehouse – the long leg of the L – formed the southern boundary. To Aaron's right, parallel to the main warehouse, an abandoned railroad spur fronted by a concrete loading dock made up the third, or northern boundary of the yard; while on the far side, straight across from Aaron, a massive, iron-banded, wooden water-tower overlooked the whole yard from the western boundary.

A tall, chain-link, prison-security style fence, which Aaron estimated to be fifteen feet high, ran under the water tower to the west and along the length of the dock to the north, enclosing the yard. It was fitted with three gates: a pair of large gates providing access to the dock and railway spur, and a single smaller gate near the water tower. Aaron could see that the two large gates were chained and padlocked, but the small gate was too far away to tell.

He leaned through the small opening, managing an arm and a shoulder before his feet slipped off the ledge and flailed through the air. His cheeks puffed out as the breath squeezed from his chest, and he struggled desperately to regain a foothold. Finally his toe caught on a wood stud and he was able to push hard with his leg and get his other shoulder through.

He paused to catch his breath, his upper body chilling in the wind, then grit his teeth, twisted and wiggled, and with an enormous final effort, popped through and flopped out onto the cold ground.

He jumped to his feet and tucked into the shadows against the high wall of cannery's north-east wing. Sweat stung his eyes and he couldn't help imagining he was playing a level in a first-person-shooter with the difficulty rating set on *insane* – mercenary soldiers hiding everywhere, ready to blast him with AK-47s. Except this game was *real*.

He worked his way down the wall of the east wing then turned and hugged the south wall. As he rounded the boiler house, which protruded from the main warehouse about two-thirds of the way down its length, he noticed a lantern burning in one of the second floor windows. He judged it to be the one in Souther's office, the window next to his desk.

Damn it, he thought, *why'd he have to choose tonight to work late ...*

Under this window, sloping all the way from just beneath it to the ground fifteen feet below, Aaron was astonished to see what appeared to be a *huge* pile of trash – like the tailings from a vast garbage mine. The disgusting obstacle filled the entire corner, where the boiler house met the cannery, and unfortunately it stood between him and the gate to freedom. In order to stay in the shadows, he would have to climb over it – a feat he quickly determined to be impossible. His only other option, short of aborting the escape and retreating to the basement, was to go around the pile, a route that would take him through the brightly moonlit area of the shipping yard, where avoiding detection would be next to impossible.

As he neared the moldering pile, he was nearly overwhelmed by a noxious stench and pulled his T-shirt collar up over his nose as a makeshift mask. Great black swarms of plump flies buzzed his head, and he jumped when an obese ship-rat dashed across his foot.

In the shadows it took a few seconds for him to make out any detail in the pile, but soon a chaotic sampling of Johnny Souther's favorite food groups came into view: Stomped beer cans, broken booze bottles, squashed soda cups, and crumpled paper napkins. Banana peels, smushed ketchup and mustard packets, half-eaten burgers, fermenting French fries, chunks of sub sandwiches, dried-up tacos, green-tinged beef burritos, and buckets of greasy chicken bones with furry potatoes.

He pushed on around the pile, hugging the shadows as long as possible, waving off flies as he went. He paused at the edge of the moon's shadow for a moment then stepped out into the moonlight.

Staying low, he managed a few encouraging steps. Then he stopped, shuddering, his stomach lurching.

In the bright moonlight he could see that the putrid drippings from this landfill horror show collected into a septic sludge river that flowed leisurely across the shipping yard, eventually sloughing off the edge of the concrete dock onto the deserted railroad tracks like the fermenting flesh from a rotting carcass. He fought off the urge to puke and quickly chose a route across. But as he toed carefully through the ooze he was startled by a distant, but clearly audible voice.

"Nice night for a moonlight stroll. Eh, kid?"

Cold fear gripped his heart, and his gaze flew to the

window high above him. Backlit by the gasoline lantern was the silhouette of Johnny Souther in his leather fedora. Aaron's luck had run out.

He made a break for the small gate under the water tower, but his feet slipped in the sludge stream and he fell hard, pain knifing through his knee, and slid on his side through the grayish goo. Up and running again, he made it to the gate, but it too was padlocked. With no time to think he began to scramble up the towering chain-link fence. His shoes, slick with muck, provided little traction, and the rough galvanized fencing pinched and sliced his muddy hands raw.

Souther took a sip from a glass of whiskey, then calmly drew his gun and took aim, sighting on Aaron as he climbed. For some reason he had taken an interest in the boy and he didn't want to kill him (at that range, with a pistol, it would be difficult not to). He hoped Aaron would simply fail to clear the fence and end the silly escape attempt on his own.

But Aaron was strong and he progressed steadily toward the top, trying desperately to ignore his bleeding hands and the gun no doubt aimed at the back of his head.

Souther steadied himself and slowly squeezed the trigger.

Just as the bullet was about to leave the chamber, Aaron encountered the coil of razor wire topping the fence, and it tore mercilessly through his clothing and into his flesh, gripping him completely. His remaining strength drained from him, and he hung from the top of the fence like a discarded stuffed animal, hopelessly entangled, expecting to be cut in two by a mercenary's AK-47 at any moment.

Souther laid down his gun, and Aaron could hear the distinct sound of applause echoing about the yard.

John Avery

-THURSDAY-

John Avery

Chapter 25

IT TAKES THREE TO TANGO

Aaron awoke with a start. He had slept hard and was cold and disoriented. He sat up and looked around then sighed heavily. He could see by the dim light of the lantern that he was back in his basement cell.

A sheet of plywood had been nailed up over the casement window, and though his instincts told him it was daylight outside, it was impossible to tell. He hauled himself up off the floor and used the coffee can to relieve himself. Then he sat on the milk crate, pulled up the hood of his sweatshirt, and took a big drink of water.

His thoughts turned to the night before. He recalled seeing Tom hit by Souther's bullet, and how the dark, cold part of his soul had been comforted by it. He could see his mother's face as she huddled with him by the fire ladder. Her trembling hands. The frightened look in her eyes. He could hear the roar of the old Nova as it whisked her off into the night, and he wondered how she was, where she was, if he would ever see her again.

He held himself responsible for what had happened that night, and he knew he alone could fix it. He'd been backed against the wall multiple times in his life and had always been able to think of a way out. But this was different. His past trials paled in comparison. He had no clever plan this time. No magic beans. He was totally at a loss. He stared at the lantern's softly glowing mantles, feeling utterly helpless and alone.

He jumped as someone unlocked the door at the top of the stairs. Johnny Souther entered and walked down the steps carrying a bag of last night's fast food leftovers. He sat down at the foot of the stairs.

"Good morning," he said, offering Aaron the food.

Aaron looked at the bag, then at his shoes. "I'm not hungry," he said, and Souther set the bag aside.

"Based upon last night's escapade," Souther said, "I'd say you're dying to get out of here."

That's the understatement of the century, Aaron thought.

"So, I thought you might like to go on a little field trip," Souther continued.

Souther's odd suggestion piqued Aaron's interest and he looked at him. "What do you mean, a field trip?"

"I have a problem, you see," Souther explained. "It takes at least three men to pull a bank job, and well, I'm a bit short handed at the moment."

Aaron paused. "I saw two men with you last night. Counting you, that's three."

"Observant," Souther said. "However, I have other business to attend to today and won't be available." He looked at his watch. "It's eight o'clock. You'll leave here in an hour."

"Why would I want to help you rob a bank?" Aaron said stupidly – he had forgotten for a moment the dire situation he was in.

Souther leaned forward and grabbed him by the jaw with a grip that might have torn off his face. "Listen, punk," he said, eyes flat. "If you think I don't know where your mother is ...

think again. I'm not asking you to help me, you little shit ... I'm telling you, okay? So shut-the-hell-up and cooperate." He released Aaron's chin with a jerk, then turned and started up the stairs. "And if I were you," he added over his shoulder, "I wouldn't fuck it up."

Chapter 26

PINK POLKA DOTS

At 8:45 a.m., Needles and Beeks readied some equipment in the cannery's main warehouse. Aaron looked on from a chair in the corner, his hands taped behind his back. He was still reeling from Souther's pep talk.

Beeks called to him. "Hey, boy. You an artist?"

"Huh?" Aaron said, surprised.

"I'm in need of an artist. You an artist or ain't you?"

"Uh, not really," Aaron said modestly, having no idea why Beeks would ask him that question. "I've done some art in school I guess ... does that count?"

"Get your puny artist-ass over here."

"He's taped to the chair, dumbass," Needles said.

"Shit ... you think I don't know that?" Beeks said, trying to hide his embarrassment. He walked over and with a flash of his knife cut Aaron's restraints then grabbed him by the shoulder with one of his big hands. "I don't have to worry 'bout you doin' nothin' stupid," he said, "do I, boy?"

"No, sir," Aaron replied, wincing under Beeks's powerful grip. He recalled how terrifyingly unreal it had felt the moment Beeks's big hand took him down to the asphalt in the alley.

Beeks had set up a makeshift workbench and stocked it with art supplies. "You think you can make me some bad-ass masks outa all this shit?" he asked. "I'm gettin' real fuckin' tired of those damn panty-hose."

Aaron paused at an image of Beeks's face smashed into a nylon stocking then blinked it away. "Uh, yeah," he replied. "I think I can handle it."

The project had caught his imagination. He took a quick inventory of the tools and supplies Beeks had laid out for him: four Styrofoam heads, four white ski masks, four colorful cans of spray paint.

"No amateur bullshit crap," Beeks insisted. "I want 'em bad-ass. You got it, boy? Bad fuckin' ass."

"No problem," Aaron said, growing more nervous now that Beeks had raised the artistic bar so high.

He stood at the workbench, rubbing the blood back into his wrists, running ideas around in his head. He thought of clown faces, but that had been done to death; horror themed masks didn't seem right to him either. He settled on a simple design he thought Beeks would like then set to work.

He stretched one of the ski masks over the first form, gave the can of electric-blue a vigorous shake, and painted a row of simple vertical stripes onto the white knit fabric head. He followed with shocking-pink polka-dots on head two, neon-green horizontal stripes on head three, and jet-black circles on head four. Then he stepped back to admire his work.

Beeks came over and tested the paint on the black mask with his finger; then he pulled it off its form. He stretched it over his glossy head and checked himself out in a mirror. One of the black circles went around the eye, like a pit bull. He smiled.

"Not bad, boy," he said, adjusting the fit, his teeth gleaming through the mouth hole. "Not too damn bad."

Aaron grinned. He couldn't remember the last time he received a compliment from anyone other than his mother, and maybe Willy.

Needles laughed at the sight of his friend. "Nice, Beeks ... really nice."

"You can kiss my big, black ass," Beeks said, still admiring himself in the mirror. "I like it fine, motherfucker. I like it just fine."

Needles selected the green horizontal stripes then tossed the pink polka-dots to Aaron.

Chapter 27

AARON GOES TO WORK

It was 9 a.m. when Beeks loaded the last of the equipment into the white van. Needles had briefed Aaron on procedure.

"You think you got it?" Needles asked.

Aaron's heart was racing in anticipation, but he had no clue what they were actually heading out to do. But it was an adventure, and he loved adventure – its mystery, its excitement, its remoteness from everyday life. "I think so," he replied, doubtfully.

"Okay," Needles said. "Let's get it done."

Needles took the driver's seat, and Beeks, still masked, rode shotgun. They pulled out and waited in the street while Aaron rolled the big door closed. He jumped into the back of the van, and when Needles hit the gas they were half way down the block before Aaron managed to get the van's side door shut.

While Needles negotiated traffic, Beeks tapped out a beat on the dashboard. He turned to Aaron and extended his hand.

"They call me Beeks," he said. "This here's Needles."

Aaron shook their hands, making sure to use a firm grip this time. "I'm Aaron," he said, grinning from ear to ear like a naive new-hire who just signed on as one of the Hole-in-the-Wall Gang.

Beeks tossed him a walkie-talkie. "Here," he said, "you're

gonna need that."

Aaron turned the radio over in his hand and recalled how he and Willy used to love to play with walkie-talkies. They would spend hours roaming the city, chatting to each other about who knows what – until Willy lost his, that is.

Needles parked the white van in front of Western Federal Bank and turned to Aaron. "Do you remember what I told you?"

Aaron went over his short list of duties list in his mind. "Yes sir," he said.

"Okay, take your position."

Aaron climbed into the driver's seat, and he and Needles pulled on their masks. Beeks pondered Souther's decision to send a young boy with them on a job.

"You think you can handle this, boy?" he asked.

Aaron peered out from behind his polka-dots. "I don't know. I'm pretty scared."

Beeks laughed. "You should be, boy. I'd be too if I was you."

"Check your radios," Needles said, and they did. "Okay ... let's move out."

Needles and Beeks shouldered their gear and entered the bank through the front entrance. Aaron stayed behind, clutching his walkie-talkie, watching the street from his seat in the van.

After ten minutes, Aaron grew restless. He checked the mirrors again and his heart jumped into his throat. A police cruiser was heading his way, and fast, lights blazing.

"Oh, *crap!*" he said, fumbling for the TALK button on his

radio. He pictured all of them being cuffed with zip ties and hauled off to jail. But the cruiser simply blew past him and turned left, away from the bank. Aaron took in a deep breath, leaned back in his seat, and exhaled slowly.

BUZZ! BUZZ! BUZZ! BUZZ! The bank's alarm had gone off. Aaron sat bolt upright and promptly dropped his walkie-talkie. "*Damn it!*" he said as he groped between the seats. He retrieved his radio and looked up just in time to see the thugs burst out of the bank dragging loaded duffel bags. He started the van then jumped in back and rolled the side door open. The thugs tossed the loot inside and jumped into the front seats.

Needles smoked the tires, and the gang made their getaway.

Beeks turned to Aaron, breathing hard. "Tell me this ain't fun, boy!" he said, flashing a huge white smile.

Aaron was totally pumped. He fist bumped Beeks and grinned ear to ear.

Riding high on the successful heist, Needles decided to make a day of it. He filled up the van at the nearest gas station, and then he and Beeks took Aaron with them on an afternoon crime spree that would have made Clyde Barrow proud.

City Heights Bank ... *robbed*.
North Park Savings and Loan ... *cleaned out*.
Bank of Nations ... *fleeced*.

Under Needles's skilled leadership, every job ran like clockwork. They finished up the day with a van load of cash and a young teenage boy whose life had, once again, been changed forever.

Chapter 28

PAY DAY

It was just after 5 p.m. when the white van rolled into the cannery. Everyone got out, and Beeks began unloading the haul.

Aaron was overflowing with adrenaline; he walked circles to contain himself. "That was incredible!" he said, high-fiving Needles. "What a rush!"

Souther had been waiting for them. He dumped the contents of one of the fat duffel bags onto a table.

Cash ... piles of it.

"Good job, boys," he said. He counted out several stacks of $100s for his thugs, then picked up a bundle of $5 bills and tossed them to Aaron.

Aaron caught the money with both hands and his eyes bugged out. "Whoa," he said. "What's this?" He figured he held $500 in his hands.

"That's your cut," Souther said, as if it were obvious.

"You're kidding," Aaron said. He certainly hadn't expected to get paid today, and $500 was more than his family's food budget for a month.

"You earned it," Souther said. "There's plenty more where that came from if you play your cards right." He stuffed the rest of the cash back into the duffel bag. "Let me know if you want to blow some of it on a whore, okay? I can arrange it."

Needles and Beeks laughed knowingly, but Aaron only gave up a sheepish grin.

Souther could back his statement up, of course, having spent countless nights over the years in the company of hookers, and he proceeded to share some of his titillating whore stories with the group.

Aaron was riveted, gripped by a raging torrent of hormones, and he lapped up every last syllable. Souther got a charge out of seeing his reactions, and he teased him with ever expanding layers of graphic detail.

Souther concluded his thrilling monologue with an anecdote that had even Needles and Beeks blushing. Then he paused – he had left out one very important detail regarding his knowledge of the business of prostitution. A secret he'd been keeping (even from Needles and Beeks) for nearly ten years, now. But he decided not to mention it – not yet at least.

"I'll bet your mother could use some cash of her own," he said at last, looking for another reaction from Aaron.

The left-field comment confused Aaron and left him feeling queasy, his enthusiasm shriveling. "What's that supposed to mean?" he said.

"Forget about it," Souther said casually. He had gotten what he wanted.

Aaron felt a sudden aversion toward the money. He tossed the bundle of bills on the table like so much rotten meat.

His cell phone lay on the table. Souther picked it up and handed it to him. "Here," he said. "I believe that's yours."

The odd gesture only served to confuse Aaron further. He searched Souther's eyes for a long moment then slipped the phone into his pocket.

Chapter 29

NO ONIONS

Michael sat on the couch in his loft, staring at a blank TV screen. He checked his watch. 7:10 p.m. He hadn't heard a word from Aaron since dropping him off at home the night before and he was deeply concerned. He pulled the slip of paper with Aaron's number on it out of his pocket and looked at it for a moment. Then he entered the number into his phone and pressed CALL.

Souther had some fast food spread out across his expansive desk. Needles and Beeks were there, and Aaron had been invited to join them.

Beeks unwrapped his cheeseburger, lifted the top bun and looked inside. He wasn't happy. "Which one of you sons-of-bitches got my damn burger?" he said.

"Chill out, Beeks," Needles said. "No one got your damn food."

Aaron felt like part of the team, now, and comfortable enough to contribute to the conversation. "Mine looks okay," he said.

Beeks scratched the onions out of his burger. "I specifically told 'em 'No damn – '"

"Shut up," Souther said, holding up his hand. "I hear something ..."

"I think it's me," Aaron said, reaching into his pocket for his phone. He didn't recognize the incoming number, but he tapped ANSWER anyway then held the phone up to his ear.

"I'll take that," Souther said, reaching across the desk, and Aaron gave up his phone.

Michael was confused by the rustling. "*Aaron?*" he said.

"Who's speaking?" Souther said.

Michael looked at his phone for a moment, then pressed END CALL.

Souther slid the phone back across the desk to Aaron.

"Who was it?" Aaron asked.

"Wrong number," Souther replied.

Michael walked over and lifted his jacket off its chair, slipping his phone into the inside pocket. But as he started for the door, he hesitated and swapped the light jacket for a heavier coat.

Souther leaned back in his chair. "Things are heating up a bit around here," he said. "Tomorrow's job is the big score we need so we can lay low for a while."

Aaron glanced at the others and listened attentively. He looked forward to the thrill of riding lookout again. And as far as he was concerned, his current earnings were already spent.

"I'll be in charge this time around," Souther continued then he looked straight at Aaron, "and you're going inside with me."

Aaron looked around to see who Souther was referring to. Beeks and Needles looked at each other and then at Aaron.

"Oh, you mean me?" Aaron said, pointing to himself. "Inside? In the bank? While you rob it?"

"While *we* rob it," Souther said. He leaned forward and

folded his hands on the desk.

Aaron knew very well that his big day of riding lookout qualified him to ride lookout – nothing more. He pictured a few of the bank robberies he had seen on TV and in movies, but he couldn't see himself playing any of the parts. The idea was totally absurd.

"But I've only been a lookout," he said. "I-I'm not ready to go inside."

"You'll be fine," Souther said, as if it happened every day. "Besides, the pay for an inside man is fifty times what it was riding lookout."

Aaron thought about that for a moment. $25,000 was an incomprehensible sum. It could mean a whole new start for him and his mom.

"Give me your phone, kid," Souther said. "What's your mother's number?"

Aaron paused, confused, and almost asked why. But instead he chose not to. It wouldn't help to argue. "She's in my contacts," he said. "Here, let me do it." He set up the call then reluctantly handed over his phone again.

Ashley lunged for her phone, catching it after the first ring. "Hello?" she said.

"Have you ever been to Sally's Diner?" Souther said.

Her heart sank – she had hoped for someone better. "No," she replied. "I don't think so."

"I want to do an exchange," Souther said.

Ashley's hand went to her mouth. She knew from Souther's inflection that he wanted more than mere ransom money. "What kind of exchange?" she asked.

"Aaron's freedom for yours."

The motel room closed in around her, and she reached for the bed as the floor fell away.

Aaron tried to grab his phone. "What are you *doing?*" he cried.

Souther touched his index finger to his lips and gave Aaron a look that made him sit down. Then he continued with Ashley.

"I believe that to be a fair exchange," he said. "Does that sound fair to you, Ashley?"

Ashley dug deep, but found nothing – she was empty. Her knees grew weak and she sat on the edge of the bed.

"Ashley?"

She placed her hand over her heart, summoning all of her will. "Yes," she said at last, her voice small and lifeless. "I think that's fair."

"Excellent," Souther said with a smile. He was pleased with how this was going.

Aaron couldn't believe what he was hearing. He reached for his phone again, but Souther turned away from him and continued his conversation.

"I'd like you to meet me at Sally's Diner tomorrow night at 6:30," he said.

Ashley could no longer contain herself. "Why meet at Sally's? Why not send one of your *goons* and just take me? You know where the hell I am."

Souther became cruelly patronizing. "You're a grown woman, Ashley. I want this to be *your* decision."

Ashley closed her eyes and touched her fingers to the bridge of her nose. *You want what to be my decision? Whether or not I kill myself?* She was tempted to refuse him, but of course there was no way she could do that. She replied slowly, scarcely breathing.

"Okay," she said. "You win. I'll be there."

Souther was deeply satisfied. He leaned back in his chair and put his feet on the desk, then looked at Aaron while he spoke to her.

"Listen carefully," he said. "If you tell anyone about this meeting ... your son dies. If you stand me up or show up late ... your son dies. If I see anyone with you at the diner ... well, I think you get my point."

Ashley felt as though she might faint at any moment. "I need to talk to Aaron," she said.

"Well, aren't you a lucky girl," Souther said with the sincerity of a veteran game show host. "He's sitting right here." He handed the phone to Aaron. "She wants to talk to you."

Aaron took the phone. "Hello?" he said.

Ashley couldn't believe it was actually him. "*Aaron?*" she said. "It's me. It's Mommy."

Tears welled in Aaron's eyes. "Don't worry, okay, Mom? I'm fine. I love you. I'll call y –"

Souther snatched the phone. "And, Ashley," he added, "don't be a fool and try to save the world or something."

Tears flowed from Ashley's eyes. She was exhausted. "Mister," she said softly, "I don't want to save the damn world ... I just want to save my little boy."

"I'll see you in twenty-four hours," Souther said coldly. Then he hung up and slid the phone back to Aaron.

Aaron was incredulous. "What was *that* all about?" he cried. "You said if I helped you my mom would be safe!"

"Oh, I didn't *mean* any of that," Souther explained. "I was just messing with her." He leaned forward and rested a patronizing hand on Aaron's knee. "You trust me, don't you, kid? I'd never want to hurt you ... or your mother."

Aaron pulled away, sickened by the evil that was Johnny Souther. "You're a liar!" he said. *"I hate you!"* He buried his face in his hands.

Souther casually wadded up the trash and chucked it out his office window. "If I were you, kid," he said darkly, "I'd choose my words a bit more carefully in the future."

Chapter 30

TARGET PRACTICE

Needles and Beeks took Aaron out of Souther's office and headed down the walkway toward the stairs. Aaron felt like he'd been hit by a truck.

Needles wanted to tell him not to worry about what Souther had said back there, but he knew Aaron wouldn't want to hear it.

Instead he turned to him and said, "Would you be interested in taking a tour of the practice range?"

Aaron looked up. "The what?"

"You know – the shooting range. Target practice. I thought maybe you could use a distraction about now."

Aaron had encountered many different shooting ranges in his video games, but he had never seen a real one. "Uh ... sure." he said. "Where is it?"

"I'll show you," Needles said. He looked at Beeks. "Are you coming with us?"

Beeks wasn't interested; he preferred to use the range alone. Besides, he had other plans. "No," he replied. "I got things I gotta do. Y'all go on without me."

Aaron had hoped he'd join them. "See ya, Beeks," he said with a little disappointed wave.

Beeks nodded and headed off to the kitchen to make a sandwich.

Needles lit a lantern, and Aaron followed him to the far

west-end of the cannery. Cut into the wood floor in an out-of-the-way first-floor corridor was a trap door held in place by two heavy iron hinges. Needles set the lantern on the floor, flipped up the large recessed pull-ring, turned it a half a turn, and yanked open the hatch.

"Ready?" he asked.

Aaron nodded.

Needles swung the heavy door over and lowered it to the floor, and then, using the lantern to light the way, he led Aaron down the steep wooden steps into a dark basement.

It's like an old ship's ladder, Aaron thought as he descended. He could only imagine what kind of crappy firing range the thugs had cobbled together in such a dark, out-of-the-way space.

"What do you use for targets?" he asked, doubtfully.

Needles was proud of the range he and Beeks had built, and he knew Aaron was in for a nice surprise. "You'll see," he replied.

Aaron stepped off the ladder onto a dirt floor and for a brief moment he thought he was back in his cell. But then Needles held the lantern high and the practice range loomed into view.

At first glance Aaron was disappointed. He naturally compared the space to the high-tech, brightly lit ranges he knew from video games. This range was tiny and as dark as a cave. The ceiling was very low; the 2 x 12 floor joists that supported the floor above ran the length of the space and they barely cleared Needles's head. Exposed electrical wiring wound between rusting cast-iron water and sewer pipes that ran in every direction.

The range had just one shooting booth and one firing lane, and the bullet trap – a wall of earth created when the cannery's foundations were dug – was a mere fifty feet away.

Not great for rifles, Aaron thought, *but okay for pistols*. He was pleased, however, to see that the range had a rudimentary target carrier system for loading fresh targets – a major convenience.

Needles stepped into the shooting booth and pulled out his 9mm pistol. He released the magazine into his palm and handed the gun to Aaron.

"Have you ever held a gun before, kid?" Needles asked, feeding shells into the magazine.

Aaron hefted the pistol and was surprised by the weight. "Not a real one," he said. He sighted down the gun's impressive gunmetal-steel barrel. "It feels really good."

"They used to recommend that you leave two or three rounds out of the magazine when not using the gun to extend the life of the spring," Needles explained. "But the newer springs are stronger, so I go ahead and top it off." He showed Aaron how to lock the magazine into the handle, and then he set the pistol aside and picked up an assault rifle.

"Okay, now pay attention," he said. "This weapon is a bit more complicated." He released the large curved magazine. "You insert the loaded magazine into the slot here below the trigger. Push it up from the bottom until the catch engages. Slap the bottom of the magazine up into the weapon to ensure that it stays, and then pull down on it to be sure."

Needles finished the demonstration and handed the rifle and magazine to Aaron. "Go ahead and try loading it."

Aaron looked the magazine over, then slid it into the

magazine-well and clicked it home. Then he slapped it hard and gave it a tug to make sure it was seated.

"Nicely done, kid," Needles said.

Aaron handed the rifle back and Needles set it aside.

"Do you want to try a few shots?" he asked.

Aaron hadn't dreamed that Needles would actually let him *shoot*. "Sure, of course," he replied, excited.

"Leave the guns where they are for a second, okay?"

"Okay."

Needles lit a second lantern and walked it down to the target end of the firing lane. He placed the lantern on a wooden shelf next to the target and adjusted its placement for the best light. Then he returned to the firing booth to show Aaron how to use the target retrieval system.

The simple system consisted of a spring-clip tied to a length of clothesline looped through two pulleys, one at each end of the firing lane, allowing the shooter to reel in the targets for inspection and replacement.

"Pull on the bottom line to bring in the target," Needles said.

Aaron pulled the rope and a tattered target with most of its bull's-eye blown away came reeling toward him. Needles selected a fresh target from a nearby stack and had Aaron clip it in place.

"Okay, now send it back down," Needles said.

Aaron pulled on the upper line, and the fresh target receded into the distance.

"You'll feel a tug when the stop-knot hits home," Needles said.

Aaron continued to pull on the rope until he felt some resistance. "I think it stopped," he said.

"Okay," Needles said. "Here, you'll want these." He handed him a pair of sound-deadening earmuffs and Aaron clamped them over his ears. Then he handed him the 9mm and showed him how to release the safety. Aaron held the gun toward the target.

"Use your other hand for support," Needles said.

Aaron wrapped his left hand around his right.

"Excellent. Go ahead and take a couple of shots."

Aaron slowed his breathing, aimed, and squeezed the trigger.

POP!

"Wow," Aaron said, looking at Needles for approval. "It has a kick."

Needles nodded. "You'll have to allow for it when you fire several shots in succession." Aaron recalled how the better video games simulated that effect.

"Go ahead," Needles said. "Fire at will."

Aaron steadied himself then fired off round after round until he emptied the gun.

"Good," Needles said. "Let's check your aim." He tugged the line and the target moved toward them. Aaron was excited to see that his shot grouping was tight around the bull's-eye.

"Nice shooting," Needles said, surprised. "*Very* nice. Do you want to try the rifle?"

"No way ... really?"

Needles took the pistol from Aaron and picked up the assault rifle. He helped Aaron place his hands in the correct positions on the weapon.

Aaron hefted it and smiled.

Needles clipped a fresh target to the string and wheeled the target down the lane into position. "You may want to rest this gun on a sandbag," he said, pulling one over. "Fire quick bursts at first to get the feel of it. It will wander on you if you're not careful. Just give the trigger a quick squeeze and release."

Aaron adjusted his earmuffs, and then he rested the barrel of the rifle on the sandbag, aimed down range, and with as much confidence as he could muster, squeezed the trigger.

POPOPOP!

The barrel kicked skyward, and three bullets splintered the wooden ceiling joists.

"Holy cow!" Aaron exclaimed, embarrassed to discover that he wasn't the marksman he thought he'd be.

Needles laughed and helped him get back into position.

Needles continued to work with Aaron until he was satisfied that Aaron could safely handle both guns.

"You're a natural," Needles said. "You could easily hold your own in a fight."

Aaron glowed; that was one of the coolest things he had ever done. "Thanks, Needles," he said. "That was awesome."

Needles smiled; he felt good about what he'd done for the boy. He extinguished the target lantern, secured everything, and led Aaron back up the steep wooden ladder to the cannery above.

Chapter 31

YOU'RE MICHAEL?

Michael drove up and skidded to a stop in front of Aaron's apartment building. He jumped out of the car and ran up the steps to ring the bell.

There was no answer.

Again.

No answer.

He located the hidden key, but when he tried it he found that the door was unlocked. He replaced the key then stepped inside, peering into the darkness of the foyer.

"Hello?" he said, clicking on a light. "Is anybody home?" A backpack lay heaped in the corner with some papers and other junk. A beach cruiser leaned against a wall.

He walked through the living room, past a set of stairs that led to the second floor, and flipped a light on in the kitchen. There was no one there, so he checked the rest of the downstairs before returning to the living room.

He climbed the stairs and about half way up his foot slipped on the carpeting and he had to put a hand down to keep from falling. As he straightened he noticed that his hand was moist. He rubbed his thumb and index finger together and felt a soapy residue that smelled like laundry detergent. He knelt and ran his hand over the carpeted stair treads. Three were damp. Then he continued on up the stairs.

The upstairs hall light was already on. Michael checked the master bedroom and bath, but they were deserted.

When he came to Aaron's room a wave of panic tightened his chest: The door was splintered by what appeared to be a gunshot to the lock. He tried the knob, but the door was still securely dead-bolted from the inside.

"Aaron?" he yelled, banging on the door. "Aaron, are you in there?"

There was no answer.

He stepped back a couple steps and lunged at the door, throwing his entire weight into it. The lock held, but the center panel had loosened and Michael was able to get his hand through and release the bolt. He swung the door open, but the room was empty. He looked out through the open window across the roof. It too was deserted.

He lingered for a moment, breathing in the cold air, thinking about Aaron. Then he left the bedroom and started back down the stairs.

As he descended he heard a sound, as if someone had dropped something in the kitchen – a plastic cup perhaps. He stopped and listened, then trotted the rest of the way down to investigate.

He entered the kitchen and noticed that the pantry door, which had been closed, was slightly ajar, now. He slowly opened it and clicked on the light.

Crouching in the shadows behind a stack of newspapers was what appeared to be a boy in a hooded sweatshirt. The boy's head was down, and Michael couldn't see his face.

"Aaron?" Michael said, but there was no reply.

He stepped over and moved some of the junk aside and was surprised to see that it wasn't Aaron at all, just a chubby little black kid wearing thick glasses.

"Come on out of there," Michael said.

Willy looked up at him, terrified. "I-I was just looking for my friend," he said, close to tears.

"It's okay," Michael said. "I'm a friend, also." He'd only known Aaron a short time, but he considered him his friend – the first friend he'd made in a long time. He offered Willy a hand up and they stepped out of the pantry.

"So, you know Aaron?" Michael said.

"I'm his best friend," Willy replied stubbornly, chin down, and with all his heart he wanted to believe it was still true. Maybe if he acted as if it were true, it would be true.

Michael pulled out a chair for Willy at the kitchen table and took a seat across from him.

"I haven't heard from him since yesterday," Michael said. "I think he's in trouble."

"To put it mildly," Willy said.

"Why? What do you know about last night?"

"I know a lot," Willy said. "I saw the whole blasted thing."

The two compared stories about Aaron's run-in with Souther and the narrow escape. Willy described their cannery hide-out and agreed to take Michael there in the morning.

Willy mentioned that he'd gone to visit Aaron's mother the evening before, and that she hadn't seen Aaron since dinner and was worried. And now she was missing, too.

"The door was unlocked when I got here," he said. "She would never do that, and I doubt Tom would either – not in our neighborhood. It doesn't make any sense. We have to find them."

Michael stood up from the table. "Come with me. I'm going to check around back." They left the kitchen, stepping outside through the side door, and headed around to the rear of the building.

A makeshift plywood-patchwork had been nailed up over what used to be Aaron's garage door. Michael and Willy entered the garage through the same small door Ashley had used.

Michael noticed a fresh pair of tire burnouts running the full length of the garage and out into the alley. He looked at Willy then knelt and slowly ran his fingers over one of the charred-rubber streaks.

They left the garage and started back up the side alley toward the street.

Michael extended his hand. "By the way, my name's Michael," he said.

Willy gave Michael's hand a vigorous shake. "I'm Willy," he said. "Bloody good to –" He stopped in his tracks. "Hey, wait a second. You're Michael? The pool table Michael? The guy with the loft? Aaron called me from your place last night."

"That was you?"

Willy nodded his head sadly. "Yes ... that was me." Then he turned and walked on up the alley.

When they reached the street in front of Aaron's apartment, Michael glanced at his watch. 7:45 p.m. "So, can I offer you a ride home? If you don't hate me, that is ..."

Willy laughed; he *had* hated the mystery Michael, but now that he had met him he could see that he really was a nice guy – and maybe he'd misjudged Aaron a little as well.

"Thanks ... but I have my bike," he said, and Michael waited while he ran inside the apartment and returned with his beach cruiser.

"So, I'll pick you up here tomorrow morning at nine?" Michael said.

"Sounds good," Willy said.

They shook hands again, and with a quick wave goodbye Willy took off toward home.

Chapter 32

A Dagwood Sandwich

Aaron poked his head through the door to the cannery break room and saw Needles sitting alone at the long wooden table with the entire contents of the refrigerator spread out in front of him. Normally the fridge was pretty bare, but that day had been a good payday, so there was plenty to eat.

Aaron started to knock on the door frame, then considered calling the whole thing off. But it was important to him – and he was probably making too much out of it anyway. *A simple question requiring a simple answer*, he told himself. So he knocked.

Needles had nearly completed the construction of a Dagwood sandwich. He turned toward the sound and smiled, bracing the wobbly stack of lunch meat with both hands.

"Aaron," he said, "come in. Are you hungry? You want some iced tea?"

"That'd be great," Aaron said. "Thank you."

Needles held the sandwich with one hand and poured Aaron a glass of tea from a surprisingly elegant crystal pitcher. He passed the box of sugar and a long spoon, and then he balanced the final slice of bread on top of his towering creation. Aaron added two spoonfuls of sugar to his tea and watched the white crystals swirl around as he stirred the amber liquid.

Needles studied his sandwich, trying to figure out the best way to eat it. "Isn't it a little late for you to be up? It must be close to midnight."

"Yeah, but I was just –"

"Do you want half of this?" Needles said, interrupting him. "I think I got a little carried away."

"Oh, sure," Aaron replied.

Needles carefully sliced the sandwich in two, then laid half on a paper plate and handed it to Aaron. "You were saying?"

Aaron paused, holding the plate in his hands; then at last he asked, "Why do you rob banks?"

Needles had already committed to a large bite and he was forced to mumble. "Because I'm an idiot," he replied, crumbs flying.

Needles's casual reaction surprised Aaron and he relaxed a bit, but he wasn't going to let him off that easy. He set his plate on the table and wiped his hands on his jeans. "No, really, why do you? I mean, it's wrong to steal ... right?"

"It's not by choice," Needles said, dodging the question intentionally this time; he was in too good of a mood to dredge up a bunch of sludge. Besides, he wasn't sure if Aaron could handle the truth.

"What do you mean?" Aaron asked.

Needles paused for a moment then decided to be up front with Aaron. "I used to be a surgeon," he said.

"Wow, really? Why'd you quit?"

"I wish I had," Needles said. "The truth is I lost everything in a lawsuit: my license, my practice, my future ... all gone in the blink of an eye."

"Oh, man," Aaron said.

"Two years ago," Needles explained, "a young child, left

unattended by his heroin-addict mother, drank some liquid drain cleaner and burned his insides out. They brought the kid to me, but he died on my operating table."

Aaron wondered how close Willy had come to doing the same thing those nights when his mother left *her* little boy all alone.

Needles slid some chips and a jar of dill pickles toward Aaron. "So, I got sued, of course, and my malpractice insurance ran out half-way through the trial. Then came the settlement with the kid's mother ..."

"Was it big?"

"Let's just say the judge wasn't sympathetic toward the 'big-city doctor.'"

Aaron leaned forward in his chair, anxious to get to the part where Needles became a bank robber. "So, what happened next?" he asked.

"Hell, I was a total wreck," Needles said. "I likely would have killed myself had it not been for Johnny Souther."

"What? You mean –"

"The same guy," Needles said. "It was Souther who loaned me the money to pay everyone off."

"You're kidding ... How much?"

"Well, after insurance, and close to a million bucks out of pocket – which left me with nothing incidentally – I owed around $475,000."

"Whoa," Aaron said. He had guessed $50,000 and thought *that* was ridiculous money.

Needles continued. "Of course I couldn't imagine how or where he would get that kind of money, but I was in no position to question him." He paused. "To this day, I still wonder where he got it. The money we make robbing banks is good, but it's not *that* good."

Just then Beeks walked in wearing a determined look on his face.

"Let me guess," Needles said to him, grateful for this unexpected chance to hassle his friend. "You're lost, and you blundered in here thinking it was the toilet."

Beeks ignored him and opened the refrigerator.

"If you don't mind, Beeks," Needles said, "we're having a private conversation here."

Beeks leaned down for a closer look at the fridge's empty shelves. "Where's all the damn food?" he asked. Then he turned and saw the huge spread Needles had laid out on the table.

Needles knew what was coming. "Easy, Jezebel. Take what you need and park your fat-ass down the road."

"Well, excuse me for bein' fuckin' hungry," Beeks said.

He gathered the food into his massive arms, wedged a drinking glass under one elbow, and hooked the pitcher of iced tea under his little finger.

"I hope you enjoy your little pow-wow while I'm out here in the damn warehouse findin' a damn table," he said, then he left in a huff.

Aaron was trying to digest Needles's wild story. He felt for Beeks; but he was happy to see that the big guy had missed the jar of pickles. He selected a large one and took a bite.

"I can't believe you borrowed that much money from Johnny Souther," he said, chewing with vigor. "Of all people."

Needles drained his iced tea in one indignant swallow. Aaron felt the atmosphere in the room become tense.

There was a long, deliberate pause as Needles calmed

himself. Why he felt compelled to explain himself to a thirteen-year-old kid, he couldn't say. "Ten years ago," he said, his voice dark and joyless, now, "Johnny Souther was my pastor."

Aaron nearly choked on his pickle.

"By the time everything with the malpractice suit happened, I had already left the church, and I hadn't seen Souther in years. But with no one else to turn to, I called him, and he agreed to meet with me. I told him about the money and he said he might be able to arrange some kind of a loan. I had no choice but to accept his terms. Of course I had no way of knowing he had just been released from prison, and unfortunately, by the time I was educated as to his current line of work I was already in up to my neck."

"It should have been obvious he was a criminal," Aaron said carelessly.

That was too much for Needles. His face turned to iron. "What makes you Mr. Big-shot expert all of a sudden? Huh? What do you know about anything? You smart-ass little shit."

He stood and started straightening up his mess, regretting ever having opened up to the boy.

Aaron was shocked and embarrassed. He had only been trying to understand and learn, and now his stomach felt as if he had eaten a handful of live snails. This strange, dark version of Needles was scary.

Silence dragged out in the room.

"Do you want to know *why* Souther left the Church?" Needles said at last, not waiting for an answer. "He didn't. He was thrown out. Nine years ago, a beautiful underage parishioner accused him of molesting her. The case went to trial, and half-way through the girl admitted she had lied about the whole affair. Souther was acquitted, but not before he'd been banned from the church, and his wife and two daughters had disowned him – taking part of his soul with them."

What Needles neglected to mention was that Souther's current, twenty-five-year-old girlfriend, Brandy Fine, and the young redhead from the church – who was sixteen and pregnant at the time of the trial – were one and the same, and that there had been a major controversy surrounding the girl's sudden reversal of testimony. Brandy had lost the baby in its fifth month and with it her ability to bear children – the news of which broke Johnny Souther's heart.

Aaron tried to speak, but nothing came out.

"So, now I'm a bank robber, too," Needles went on, "and there ain't a damn thing I can do about it. I'm sorry I can't live up to your lofty ideal ... t-to your image of a *perfect* world full of *perfect* people."

Aaron stared at his hands. "I'm sorry I upset you, Needles," he said, genuinely sorry he had started a fight.

Needles wiped his hands on a paper towel. "Not everyone is born with the same level of decency, you know – sometimes you're forced to adapt. Your hallowed concept of right and wrong may have to bend, or even break, and you may find yourself abandoning your morals simply to survive." He tossed the paper towel in the sink. "If I can stay alive and out of prison for six more months, I'll have Souther paid off – and if I survive a year, I'll have enough to retire. Maybe *that* would make you happy."

Aaron hated to be misunderstood, especially when it hurt someone's feelings. "I wasn't trying to judge you, Needles," he said. "I was –"

143

"Oh, please ..." Needles said, cutting him off. He'd had enough.

"No, really," Aaron said. "I like you. You and Beeks are my friends. For the first time in my life I feel like I'm part of a team. I don't care if I ever go home."

"You make me want to puke," Needles said, lowering his head in disbelief. "One afternoon of text book heists and you conclude that the life of a goddamn bank robber is all glamour and excitement. We had fun, right? Every job was duck soup, right? Well, guess what? Tomorrow Johnny Souther will be in charge, and boy are you in for a surprise – one *huge* fucking surprise."

He slammed a cupboard shut and started for the door. "I need some sleep," he said. "We leave here at 9 a.m. sharp."

Then he walked out of the room.

-FRIDAY-

John Avery

Chapter 33

JUMPSUITS

The gang met as planned at 9 a.m. in the cannery's main warehouse. They gathered their gear together and loaded up the black van.

Aaron could feel the tension in the air; he and Needles had barely spoken. He started to have second thoughts, but he kept telling himself why he was doing this: for his mom and the money that would rebuild their lives.

Beeks pulled some white painter's jumpsuits and some thin black-leather gloves out of a duffel bag and handed each of them a set.

Aaron's jumpsuit was three sizes to big; it bagged around his shoes, and it took a minute for him to locate his hands so that he could roll up the cuffs enough to walk.

Everyone climbed into the van, with Beeks at the wheel and Johnny Souther at shotgun. Needles and Aaron sat in back with the gear, and as they drove away from the cannery, Aaron was unable to see the tungsten silver Aston Martin pulling up in front of the cannery.

Chapter 34

THEY'LL BE BACK

Michael parked the Aston near the big roll-up door.

"This car is incredible!" Willy said as they got out. He placed his hand on a roof so low that even he could see over the top.

"You know what?" Michael said. "You're a bright young man. I'll bet someday you'll own one just like it."

Willy smiled. He thought that sounded just fine. "It's over here," he said, then walked over and pulled aside the sheet metal covering the secret entrance.

Michael checked the street then followed him inside.

Pinstripes of dusty sunlight wrapped the high interior walls. The quiet was complete.

"I don't think anyone's here," Willy whispered, unnerved. The air was very warm, and as he tugged off his sweatshirt he saw that Aaron's BMX bike still leaned against the same wooden post where he had left it. He walked to it and draped his jacket over the seat.

There was a plain white van parked in the warehouse; they checked it, but it was empty.

They searched the rest of the main floor and then outside in the shipping yard and the boiler house, but Aaron was nowhere to be found. They went back inside and climbed the rough stairs to the cannery's second floor.

They checked the maintenance room, but it was empty.

They tried the office, and Michael found a soft drink cup with a ring of condensation around its bottom edge. He thumbed off the lid and saw a few small pieces of ice floating in the bottom.

"Someone was here," he said, "and not too long ago."

Willy looked at Michael with fear growing in his spectacled eyes. "Do you think they have Aaron?"

"I don't know. Probably."

"Do you think they'll come back?"

"Yes, Willy, they'll most certainly be back."

They left the cannery and agreed to meet again later in the day.

Michael dropped Willy off at his home and drove off in search of Aaron – hoping he might get lucky this time.

Chapter 35

SMOOTH

The black van circled the block under cover of heavy rains and fog that darkened the downtown neighborhood of Community Plaza Bank. When Souther was satisfied, he directed Beeks to park just down the street from the front entrance. Beeks pulled up to the curb and killed the engine.

Souther glanced at the bank's large clock. 9:25 a.m.

Aaron listened to the rain pattering on the roof of the van, his heart in his mouth. Random thoughts bounced around in his head like bingo balls, and whenever he managed to grab one, it was either too depressing to contemplate, or it made no sense whatsoever. One by one he tossed them back in the hopper with the others.

His eyes went wide, as Souther opened the glove box and pulled out a fifth of whiskey.

Great, Aaron thought, *I get to rob a bank with a bunch of drunks.*

"To a successful heist," Souther said, unscrewing the cap. He took a huge swig and passed the bottle to Beeks. Beeks took an even bigger drink and passed the bottle to Aaron.

Aaron passed the bottle to Needles without drinking.

"Wait a minute," Souther said. "Let the kid have a drink."

"Oh, no thanks," Aaron said, blushing. "I've never drank alcohol before."

Souther laughed. "Go ahead," he insisted. "You're a tough guy, right?"

Aaron hadn't ever thought of himself as a tough guy, and his experience with Tom had soured him on whiskey. But he was certainly curious, and the thought of drinking with the men excited him. Besides, it was a welcome distraction.

"I guess one small drink won't hurt," he said.

He took the bottle in both hands, raised it to his lips, and tried to take a small sip. But as he tilted his head back, the whiskey sloshed forward in the bottle and about four shots flushed down his throat and up his nose. He lurched forward, nearly dropping the bottle, and coughed so deeply his eyes nearly blew out of their sockets.

His world grew dark as colorful paisley patterns flashed about in a sea of black tea. The gang could only laugh while he coughed and snorted, his ears glowing bright red as the fiery spirits ignited his sinuses. He had never snorted gasoline through a straw and held a match to it before, but now he knew how it would feel.

Finally a flood of tears signaled the end of the worst, and Aaron looked up at the others. "Holy crap," he croaked, trying to catch a breath. He wiped the tears from his cheeks and the drool from his chin as a burning warmth welled in his stomach and heated the back of his head.

"What do you think, kid?" Souther asked, still laughing. "Smooth, right?"

"Right," Aaron wheezed.

The bottle went around again, but this time when the whiskey came to him, Aaron passed it on.

Chapter 36

NOTHING BUT A SMILE

Souther put the bottle back in the glove box then stepped out onto the sidewalk and rolled the van's side door open.

Needles climbed out, then leaned in and dragged a particularly bulky duffel bag toward him and pulled out three assault rifles, a 9mm pistol, two smoke bombs, and a small, old-fashioned kitchen timer. He handed Souther and Beeks each a rifle and took the third rifle and the two smoke bombs for himself.

Souther laid his rifle on the front passenger seat and picked up the 9mm. He released the magazine into his gloved palm, topped it off with bullets and clicked it back into the handle. He set the pistol on the floor of the van and went through the same routine with the assault rifle.

Aaron watched all of this with interest and blurred vision. He had seen Needles and Beeks carrying guns with them into the banks they robbed, but he hadn't been inside to see how they used them.

"Why do we need guns, anyway?" he asked, thinking about it.

Souther picked up the kitchen timer and slipped it into one of his pockets. "You can't rob a bank with nothing but a smile, kid," he said, then added, "but don't get any ideas about carrying one yourself."

Beeks handed out Aaron's colorful ski masks. Souther removed his fedora, pulled on his blue vertical stripes and replaced the hat. Needles donned the green horizontal stripes and Aaron his familiar pink polka-dots. Black circles again, Beeks stayed at his assigned post in the driver's seat. He clicked on his radio and made himself comfortable.

Needles grabbed four empty duffel bags and a large black-plastic trash bag from the back of the van. He handed the trash bag to Aaron, and a quick radio check completed the gang's preparations.

"It's show time, boys," Souther said. Then he and Needles shouldered their rifles and, without waiting for Aaron, trotted down the block toward the bank.

As Aaron scrambled out of the van to join them, his hand landed on the 9mm pistol left lying on the floor. He looked at Beeks – who was watching the street, radio at hand – then slipped the pistol into a pocket of his jumpsuit.

He leaped out of the van, slammed the side door shut, and double-timed it down the block through the rain to catch up.

The big clock read 9:30 a.m.

John Avery

- PART TWO -

The Big Job

John Avery

Chapter 37

TRICK-OR-TREAT

... 9:40 a.m.

Aaron removed his hands from his ears and glanced around the room. It was as if a bomb had gone off: teller windows shattered; desks and chairs overturned and riddled with bullet holes; two dozen hostages flat on their stomachs, covered with debris.

He stood, bones buzzing with adrenaline, and had to fight the urge to laugh. Here he was, in the middle of a bizarre, violent, life threatening situation, and he was *getting into it.* For a few precious moments nothing else in his turbulent adolescent world existed.

Souther and Needles reloaded and surveyed the hostages.

"Okay, listen up!" Souther said. "Which one of you idiots knows the combination to the vault?"

Silence.

"I didn't bring a damn can-opener, people!" Souther shouted. "Who has the combination to the fucking safe?"

The hostages glanced at one another, but no one dared speak.

Souther grit his teeth and fired, flipping a random hostage violently onto his back where he lay dead. The other hostages screamed and recoiled in horror.

Aaron's lungs seized up, as if a cement truck had backed up over his chest. He sank to his knees as his brain, succumbing to a neuron overload, switched off.

Needles held his position.

"You'd better hope the combination didn't die with that guy," Souther yelled.

Amidst the chaos, a lone hostage cried out. "I have it! I know the combination! God, please ... I'm the one ..."

The others continued to scream and moan.

Souther fired another three-round burst into the ceiling. "Would you shut the hell up?" he shouted, and a heavy hush lay over the room.

A frail, middle-aged man with wire-rimmed glasses got cautiously to his feet and raised his hands, trembling inside his three-piece suit. On his name tag: BANK MANAGER.

"And who are you?" Souther asked.

"I-I'm the manager," the man said.

"I got that, you idiot. What's your *name?*"

"Oh, uh – it's Walden ... J-Jim Walden."

"And how long have you been manager here, Jim?"

"I-uh – seventeen ... yes ... s-seventeen years next month."

"Okay, Jim," Souther said. "Go with him." He gestured toward Needles.

Needles patted Jim down and had him gather up the empty duffel bags. Then he took him at gunpoint and headed for the basement vault.

"Okay, everyone!" Souther said. "My young friend here will accept your donations, now." He indicated Aaron.

Still short of breath and barely lucid, Aaron struggled to his feet and pulled the plastic trash bag out of his jumpsuit pocket. He held it open and stared out at his audience. The abject terror in their eyes mirrored his.

"Everything goes in the bag." Souther said. "That includes

cell phones, people!"

Aaron moved from hostage to hostage like a battery-powered Halloween robot playing a sick game of trick-or-treat. Ladies surrendered their jewelry and purses, men their watches and wallets, their tortured souls reaching out to Aaron like diseased prisoners clawing the dungeon turnkey.

The massive stainless-steel vault door was circular and about eight feet in diameter. It was polished to a mirror finish, with a large brass-spoked handle in its center.

Jim was hunched over the fluted dial, betting his life on completing his assigned task. His hands shook, and he dripped with sweat. He peeled his glasses from his face and wiped them dry with his handkerchief.

Needles prodded him in the back with his rifle barrel. "Let's go," he said. "I could've opened the damn thing myself, by now."

"I'm trying," Jim said. "God in heaven ..." He replaced his glasses and continued to tickle the sensitive dial. "I-I just need the last ... lousy ..."

He stood and proudly spun the handle, then pulled hard against the weight and swung the massive door aside.

"Okay, let's *move,*" Needles said, gesturing with the barrel of his gun. Then he followed Jim into the vault.

Aaron's trash bag was getting heavy; he pictured it ripping wide open and wondered what he would do if it did.

He came upon the dead hostage – the frozen expression of death by surprise. Aaron tried to lift the bulky bag over the sizable pool of blood that had spread into the surrounding carpet, but the thin black plastic just stretched and dragged through the blood, leaving a crimson trail as he passed.

The blue smoke effect was rapidly dissipating as Souther paced the floor in the center of the lobby, his rifle hanging in one hand, his eyes and teeth flashing through the holes in his ski mask.

"Let's be generous, shall we?" he said. "A wedding ring is not worth your fucking life."

Jim Walden appeared from the back dragging four heavy duffel bags; he was soaked to the skin with sweat and looked to have aged ten years. Needles followed, a stride behind, the barrel of his rifle making a dent in Jim's back.

Souther was openly pleased. "I'll take those," he said.

Jim slid the straps off of his narrow shoulders and the money slumped to the floor at Souther's feet.

"Go join the others," Souther said.

Jim nodded and did as he was told. As he passed the dead hostage, he paused to spread his suit jacket over the victim's face.

Souther saw that Aaron was finishing up as well. He pulled the little kitchen timer out of his jumpsuit pocket, set the dial to five minutes, and placed it on the carpet between the empty smoke canisters. Then he stepped back and looked around at the hostages.

"Listen up!" he shouted. "When that bell rings you are free to go about your business." He indicated the timer. "Until then, stay where you are and no one else gets hurt."

He and Needles gathered up their loot and headed for the door. Aaron brought up the rear, dragging his bag behind him.

Suddenly he stopped, let go of the bag, and pulled the gun out of his pocket.

"*I QUIT!*" he screamed, and a deafening silence absorbed

his words like a padded coffin.

Souther turned to see the barrel of his 9mm pointing straight at him. He recalled having left the gun on the floor of the van and kicked himself for being an idiot.

"Nice move, kid," he said calmly. "What's going on?"

The enormity of Aaron's predicament burst upon him like a thunderclap and his heart dropped into his shoes.

This monster would just as soon kill me right now as wipe his nose, he thought. *But I can't just shoot him – can I? Oh, God ... what have I done ...*

His thoughts trailed off. Time slowed and the pistol grew heavy in his hands. For a brief torturous moment he considered turning the gun on himself. Then he began to cry.

"I can't do this any more," he said. "I can't do this to these people."

"It's just stuff, kid," Souther said, sounding coldly imperious. "They'll get over it."

Aaron held the gun steady. "That's *bullshit!*" he shouted. "They won't get over it! One of them is dead because of you! You murdered him!" He quickly wiped his eyes with the arm of his jumpsuit, knocking his ski mask slightly askew. "Do you know what I think? I think you're nothing but a big bully! You act tough all the time to cover up the fact that inside you're a coward – a blood-thirsty psycho who kills people because he can't think of a better way to get things done!"

Souther took a slow, deep breath, removed his hat, and held out his hand. "Hand over the gun, kid," he said.

"No! I won't!" Aaron cried. "Give it back! Give all the money back!" He tried to kick his trash bag away, but it was too heavy and his shoe simply crunched into the contents.

A crackle over the radios made him jump.

"*Time to rock, motherfuckers!*" Beeks said in a distorted walkie-talkie voice.

"Copy that," Needles replied, keeping his rifle on the hostages.

"Come on, kid," Souther said. "The cops will be –"

"Give it back!" Aaron cried. He took aim at Souther's forehead with a deadly two-handed grip. *"ALL OF IT!"*

"Okay, kid ... take it easy," Souther said. "I'm giving it back." He slowly lowered his duffel bags to the floor. "Look ... Here's the money ... I'm giving it back." One of the bags fell open and a few stacks of $100 bills spilled out onto the carpet.

"You, too, Needles!" Aaron said with a wave of his pistol.

Needles eased the bags off of his shoulder.

"Okay, now get the hell out of here!" Aaron said.

"No problem, kid," Souther said. "You can put away the gun. We're leaving ..." He took a couple of steps back, then turned to leave. "Let's go," he said to Needles.

Needles gave Aaron a look that said, *I hope you know, kid, you're digging a hole you can't easily un-dig, here.* Then he stepped over the empty smoke canisters and followed Souther across the trashed lobby toward the door.

Aaron lowered his weapon and looked at the hostages. His ski mask was soaked with tears. They looked at him like he had just descended from heaven.

He found himself oddly amused by the hellish absurdity of his situation and nearly laughed out loud. Then a morbid chill ran through him and he thought, *Is this what it feels like to go insane?*

Suddenly the little timer bell went *DING!*

Souther swung around in the doorway and fired a single

shot.

Aaron staggered back, dropped the gun, and gripped his chest. He looked at Souther, at Needles, at the hostages, blinking through his eye holes like a World War I recruit who's discovered that his gas mask has a leak. He looked down and sucked a quick breath in through his teeth. A heavy flow of dark red blood oozed from between his black-leather knuckles and dripped on the rolled-up cuffs of his white jumpsuit. *Oh, god*, he thought; then his eyesight flooded red, then black, and he lost consciousness before hitting the floor.

Needles ran and knelt at Aaron's side, screaming at Souther. "You fucking son-of-bitch! You shot him! You shot the goddamn kid!"

The hostages were hysterical.

Souther fired a quick burst over their heads. "Anyone else want to be part of the show?" he shouted, trying to maintain control.

Needles laid down his rifle and checked Aaron's pulse.

Souther shouldered the duffel bags and rifles. "Let's get the fuck out of here, man!" he yelled. Panic teased at him and the walls of the bank started to close in on him.

Needles unzipped his white jumpsuit, stripped to his undershirt, and packed Aaron's wound with his shirt. He lifted Aaron enough to see that the bullet had passed cleanly through the shoulder. Then he packed the exit wound as well. Finally he yanked off his undershirt and wrapped it tightly around Aaron's chest, completing the makeshift bandage.

BUZZ! BUZZ! BUZZ! BUZZ! Jim Walden had triggered the bank's alarm.

"Leave the kid, damn it!" Souther shouted over the din. "We gotta fucking bounce, man!"

Needles looked up at Souther. "Aaron is right. You are a fucking coward." He gathered the boy up in his arms. "And we aren't leavin' him ..."

Thunder and drenching rain pounded the robbers as they exited the bank – Souther with the money bags and assault rifles, Needles naked to the waist with the dying boy in his arms. Beeks was ready with the engine running; he spotted them and sped forward to pick them up. Everyone loaded into the van and Beeks spun the tires on the wet pavement as they swerved off down the street.

In the distance, *sirens* ...

Chapter 38

DOCTOR IN THE HOUSE

Beeks drove hard, heading south, in the direction of the cannery. His worried eyes filled the rear view mirror.

"What's goin' down, bro?" he asked Needles.

"The kid got shot," Needles replied from the back of the van.

"You're shittin' me ... What kinda piece-of-shit son-of-a-bitch asshole would shoot a damn –"

"Shut up and drive," Souther said.

Needles carefully removed Aaron's ski mask and stroked the boy's matted hair back from his face. He tucked a folded duffel bag under Aaron's head and sprinkled a few drops of water onto his dry lips.

The black van pulled into the cannery and skidded to a stop. Beeks jumped out and ran around to open the rear doors. Needles helped him take Aaron into his arms.

Souther dragged a leather briefcase out of the van and started for the door. "You should have left him," he said. "He's dead either way."

"Bring him into the break room," Needles told Beeks, ignoring Souther. "We have to move fast."

Beeks cradled the boy in his huge arms and followed Needles. "What're you gonna do with him in there?" he asked.

165

"I'm a doctor. What do you think I'm going to do with him?"

"What the hell you talkin' 'bout? You ain't no damn doctor."

Souther stepped out onto the sidewalk and rolled the big steel door closed behind him.

Chapter 39

THE BLUE DOOR

Souther walked four blocks east along the waterfront before turning two blocks north. He arrived at a small, gray, two-story building with no windows and a single royal blue entry door. Above the door was a small black sign with white lettering that read BLACK EAGLE STUDIOS. The door was secured with a hasp and heavy padlock. Souther removed a small brass key from his briefcase and unlocked the lock. Then he stepped inside, leaving the door ajar.

A pair of shiny black sedans were parked nearby. From the first car emerged four beautiful teenage girls dressed in provocative attire; from the second stepped a striking redhead in her middle twenties. She tossed her long flaming hair back from her face and checked the street. Then together the ladies followed Johnny Souther inside and closed the blue door behind them.

Chapter 40

THE E.R.

The thugs slammed through the door into the cannery break room.

"Over here," Needles said, clearing the large wooden table with one long sweep of his arm.

Beeks laid Aaron gently down on the makeshift operating table. Needles lit a gasoline lantern, placed it for optimum light, then checked the unconscious boy's pulse.

"I think he's dyin'," Beeks said.

"I'll be the one that says who's dying," Needles said. "Boil some water."

"What? How much?"

"A pot full, you idiot. Don't you watch any movies?"

"More than you, motherfucker," Beeks said. He found a pot and set some water to boil. Needles positioned two more lamps.

"Where the hell did Souther go?" Beeks asked.

"How should I know ... home to Brandy Fine, I suppose." He paused. He hadn't seen Souther's girlfriend in over a year and was curious as to why she suddenly came to mind. "Who gives a damn, anyway?" he said at last.

"Well, excuse me for makin' conversation," Beeks said.

Needles yanked open a cupboard and slid out a large shoebox. He spread out a clean towel, removed the lid from the shoebox, and dumped the contents. Out spilled an array of surgical equipment: scalpels, scissors, forceps, clamps, suturing materials, sponges, masks, miscellaneous bottles, bandages and hypodermic needles.

He sorted through the items. "Did anyone ever tell you you talk too much?"

"No ... maybe you, I guess," Beeks said.

"Well, you do."

"Fuck you."

Needles unwrapped the blood-soaked bandages, unzipped Aaron's jumpsuit, and tore open his sweatshirt and shirt. It was an upper-chest wound, the bullet having passed through Aaron's body just under his left collar bone. Fresh blood pooled on the wooden tabletop and dripped onto the white porcelain floor tiles.

Needles carefully rolled Aaron up onto his side then grabbed some clean paper towels and applied pressure to the wounds.

He saw Beeks's stomach lurch. "What's the matter, Beeks?" he goaded. "You've seen blood before."

"I seen plenty of blood," Beeks said. "More than you, I'll wager." He paused. "Well ... maybe not more than you ... but I seen a lot."

"So, what's your problem?"

"What's *your* problem?"

"I'm not the one with the problem."

"Fuck you."

Needles got Aaron's bleeding under control and was encouraged to see that the bullet had entered and exited his body relatively cleanly, with little apparent damage to the underlying tissue. He splashed antibiotic solution over the wounds and covered them with sterile gauze.

He checked his watch. 11:30 a.m. Then he looked at Beeks impatiently. "Well?"

Beeks looked back at him ... puzzled.

"My water ... ?"

"Oh ..." Beeks said. He checked the pot. There were small bubbles forming in the bottom. "It's comin'."

"Well, hurry it up."

"How the fuck do you hurry water?"

"How should I know," Needles said. "Figure it out." He scrubbed up in the sink. "Wash up. I'm gonna need your help."

"No way, bro," Beeks said, raising his big hands in the air in protest. "You know I don't know nothin' about no medical shit."

"Do you see anyone else in this room that hasn't been shot?"

"Kiss my ass."

Beeks washed up, then checked his pot of boiling water. "I think we're good here," he said, and Needles came over and plunged his tools into the bubbling liquid.

He spread some clean towels out on the table next to Aaron then selected two surgical masks from the shoebox pile.

"Put this on," he said, handing one to Beeks, "and if Aaron wakes up ... hold him. You got that? You hold him good!"

Beeks pulled on his mask and adjusted the undersized nose piece. It made him sound like he had a cold. "If he does wake up I hope he don't see you first."

"And why is that?"

"'Cause you're so damn ugly ... you'd probably scare the poor son-of-a-bitch to death."

Needles had to laugh. "Good one, friend," he said.

He found some surgical gloves in a Ziploc bag and looked doubtfully at his assistant's enormous hands; still Beeks somehow managed to pull on a pair without ripping them to pieces.

The big black man walked over and stood next to the mutilated boy; the kid seemed so small lying there on that big table. "I gotta bad feelin', bro," he said.

"Let's just get on with it," Needles said. He prepared a shot of morphine and set it aside.

"You got morphine? Shit, man ... boot him up!"

"Thanks for the expert advice," Needles said, "but I want him to be as awake as possible – too much morphine at this stage could kill him." He reached for a pair of forceps. "Now, shut your yap and give me a sponge."

He infiltrated the area with an anesthetic solution, then clamped the sponge into the forceps and began to clean the wounds.

Aaron was beginning to regain consciousness and he jerked violently after a particularly deep probe.

"Hold him ..." Needles said.

Beeks leaned in and put his weight into it. "Bang the son-of-a-bitch, man ..."

"Not yet," Needles said, redoubling his efforts. "Just another minute ..."

Another deep probe and Aaron screamed. Beeks looked at Needles like he was some sort of sadistic Nazi.

"I know, okay?" Needles said, reaching for the prepared syringe. He injected the morphine directly into a vein on the inside of Aaron's arm and monitored the boy's pulse as he drifted back into semi-consciousness.

Needles finished with antibiotic ointment and clean, dry-gauze bandages. Then he stepped back and pulled off his gloves, exhausted by the effort.

"Is he gonna live?" Beeks asked doubtfully.

"It's hard to say," Needles replied. "The bullet passed through cleanly and missed his lung – and no bones or large vessels were hit ... but he lost a lot of blood. We'll have to see."

Beeks gathered Aaron up in his arms and carried him to the sofa and laid him down. Needles wiped down the operating table with soapy rags and dropped them into a trash bag along with the blood soaked towels. He walked over to where Beeks was sitting on the sofa with the boy. Beeks had covered Aaron with a blanket. Needles tucked it up under the boy's chin.

"Why do you care so much 'bout this boy, anyways?" Beeks asked, genuinely curious.

Needless looked at Beeks, then at Aaron, and thought for a moment. "I'm not quite sure ..."

"I knows the feelin'," Beeks said.

"Maybe it's because that's what doctors do," Needles said. "Or maybe it's because in today's world, good people are in short supply."

He checked his watch. 1 p.m. Then he laid his hand on Aaron's head and said, "Sleep well my young friend."

Chapter 41

MORPHINE SULPHATE

The sun was slowly melting in the west, and the huge steel-sided cannery glowed, as if it had been heated to a high temperature. Willy rode up and skidded to a stop out front. He peeked in through the secret entrance and listened for a moment ... then ducked inside, pulling his bike in after him.

As he had hoped, his sweatshirt still lay over Aaron's bike seat where he left it. He grabbed it, and as he turned to leave he heard a faint moaning sound that sent a chill through him. He stopped and listened ... but as quickly as it had come, it was gone. His best guess was that the sound had come from the break room, so he stepped quietly over to investigate.

He peered into the room, straining to see in the limited light. It appeared to be vacant. But as he turned to go he saw something that made the hair on his arms stand on end. Shoved up against one wall was the familiar old maroon-velvet sofa, but lying prone along its length he saw a shadowy figure. Panic leaped in him, accelerating his heartbeat, and he breathed in deeply, fighting off a strong urge to turn and run.

He took a step closer to the mysterious form and refocused his eyes. To his astonishment he saw that the ominous death figure on the couch was none other than his best friend, Aaron Quinn.

Willy lit a lantern and set it on the table. Aaron appeared to be asleep, and, in the lamplight, looked even more frightening than he had in the dark. Willy knelt at his side and spoke to him in a low, cautious voice.

"Aaron?" he said. "Aaron, it's me ... it's Willy. Are you okay?"

Aaron didn't budge. Willy put his ear to Aaron's lips and detected a wisp of breath. He gently stirred him with his finger. Aaron slowly opened his eyes, and at that moment there was no one on earth he would have rather seen. He reached out his hand to his friend and spoke just above a whisper.

"Willy ..."

Willy squeezed Aaron's hand and said, "You're one butt-ugly bugger, you know."

Aaron wanted to laugh, but only smiled. He was in agony. "It hurts bad, Willy."

Willy noticed Aaron's bandaged shoulder peeking out from under the blanket. He eased the blanket down a few inches and the extent of the damage came into view.

"What in bleeding hell happened to you?" he asked.

Embarrassed, Aaron hesitated then replied bluntly, "I got shot."

Willy hesitated. "*Shot ... ?"* he cried. "Damn it, Aaron ... I saw you escape from that guy. What happened? Did he come after you?"

Aaron paused, his head throbbing. It was difficult for him to recall the correct sequence of events.

At last he said, "We were robbing a bank, and I –"

"Wait a second ... Did you say you were *robbing a bank?*"

"Yes," Aaron replied sheepishly.

Willy wanted to scream. "*What?*"

Aaron fought back tears as his shameful confession poured out. "I joined up with them, Willy. They kidnapped me ... a-and I tried to escape ... then my mom called ... and I joined their gang and made masks ... a-and we drank whiskey and robbed Community Plaza Bank in jumpsuits – and they shot me."

This was too much for Willy. He forgot all about Aaron's weakened condition and laid into him. "You stupid sod," he said. "I heard about that robbery ... someone *died* during that!"

Aaron knew this, of course. "I know," he admitted sadly.

"I can't believe this is happening," Willy said looking around. "You've done some barmy-ass shit before, Aaron. But this – this takes the bloody freakin' cake."

He turned and took a few steps away ... then returned. "You know what? If you don't die from being shot, I'll kill you myself." He went to the sink for a glass of water. He was totally knackered.

Aaron wanted desperately for Willy to understand and forgive him. "I don't know how I got mixed up in all this," he said. "But it happened, okay? ... and I'm sorry. I'm really, really sorry."

"You should be," Willy said gruffly, his back to Aaron. *"Shit ..."*

Aaron glanced at the clock over the stove. 5:30 p.m. He tried to sit up, but it hurt too much and he flopped back down clenching his teeth.

"I have to go to Sally's Diner tonight," he said, sweating, now.

"Yeah, right," Willy said, uninterested. "You can't even sit up."

Aaron felt himself entering the early stages of panic. He made two fists, struggling to keep his head clear. "I have to do something," he said, "or he'll kill her."

Willy turned and looked at him. "What the bloody hell are you talking about? Kill who?"

"My mom!"

"What? Who will?"

"Damn it, Willy ... don't you ever listen? *Johnny Souther!* The guy I robbed the damn bank with. The guy who *shot me* for cryin' out loud." He coughed hard into his hand, and there was blood. "They're meeting at Sally's Diner tonight at 6:30. *She's trading herself for me!*"

He pointed urgently at a small plastic trash can sitting on the floor under the table. Willy grabbed it and handed it to him. Aaron clutched the container to his chest and wretched. Then he continued.

"She's seen his face, Willy. She saw him kill Tom. He'll hurt her. I know he wants to hurt her!" He began to shiver and Willy pulled the blanket up to cover him.

"Here, try to drink," Willy said, trading the trash can for the glass of water.

Aaron managed a few sips, then wiped his mouth and eyes on his sleeve and gathered himself for a moment.

"I think we should take the son-of-a-bitch *out*," he said at last.

"Whoa!" Willy coughed, unprepared for that one. "Let's slow down a minute ..." He glanced around for Aaron's trash can, feeling a strong urge to donate some of his own vomit to the cause.

Aaron looked at him, eyes full of fear, the pain intense. He couldn't think of any other way out of this. "What else can I do, Willy?" he argued. "*What else can I do ... ?*"

Willy took a drink from the water glass, struggling to find his words.

"Listen, mate," he said at last, placing his hand on Aaron's arm. "Try and get some rest, okay?" Then, with false confidence, he added, "I'll think of something ..."

Aaron nodded and relaxed a little, then laid his head back and closed his eyes.

Willy was at a loss. He wandered through the kitchen, absently opening cabinets in the hope of triggering an idea. He came across a large curious shoebox, which he promptly removed from its shelf. He set the box on the table and pulled off the lid – it looked like the inside of a doctor's medical bag.

Among the many items packed into the box were several small pill bottles. Willy picked one of them up and checked the label: *Morphine Sulfate - Sustained Release Tablets, 15 mg.*

He recalled, as a child, seeing similar bottles in his mother's medicine cabinet, and had since read up on morphine's dangerous, yet superior pain-killing properties. He shook two tablets out into his hand, then went over and knelt next to Aaron.

"Aaron ..." he said softly, as not to startle him. "Put these under your tongue."

Aaron opened his eyes and looked at the suspicious pills. "What are they?"

"It's morphine."

"*Morphine?* Where the hell'd you get morphine?"

"Someone left a shoebox full of medical crap in the cupboard," Willy explained. "There's a ton of it in there.

You've probably been whacked out on the stuff for hours."

Aaron made a face, then placed the tablets under his tongue and took a sip of water.

"Have a bit of a rest," Willy said, comforting him. "You'll be nickers in half an hour." He pulled up a chair next to his friend.

Aaron closed his eyes and fell asleep.

Chapter 42

SAND CASTLE MAGIC

At 5:46 p.m. Aaron abruptly sat up, like an awakening corpse, scaring Willy half to death. He opened his eyes, but Willy wasn't sure they were seeing him. Aaron mumbled a few syllables of nonsense and flopped back down. Willy tucked the blanket up under his chin and waited.

Aaron's mother pulled back the lace curtains, letting the rising sun shine through his leaded-glass bedroom window. The sun seemed to shine right through her, and she glowed like something from heaven.

He got out of bed and looked out across the rooftops of a strange but wonderful world. It was as if he'd gone back in time a 150 years – to old England perhaps – and yet he wasn't surprised by it. He felt refreshed and wonderful.

His mother smiled at him.

"Am I asleep?" he asked.

"Only if you wish to be," his mother replied.

He walked down a grand staircase into a spacious, marble-floored entry hall. Priceless antiques, furniture and paintings adorned the room.

Aaron's father, Danny Quinn, stood by the hand-carved front door with the fingers of one hand tucked into his vest pocket and the others holding a gold pocket watch. The war medals around his neck gleamed as sunlight struck off of their polished detail.

He smiled at Aaron and opened the door for him. "We've been expecting you," he said.

"Am I dreaming?" Aaron asked.

"Only if you wish to be," his father replied.

Aaron shook his father's hand firmly then stepped through the front door to the outside.

Where his front porch and the crumbling concrete steps should have been there was now a stretch of beach running right up to the threshold. Aaron stepped out onto the warm white sand and enjoyed the sensation as it moved between his bare toes. He scooped up a handful and let it run slowly through his fingers.

A young black boy was sitting in the sand nearby. He was building a fantastic sandcastle. Aaron had never seen such wonderful attention to detail. The stone walls and corbeled corner turrets looked stunningly real. The boy had even dredged a moat around the perimeter of the castle and filled it with seawater to slow marauders. The drawbridge was a chunk of flat driftwood, and the boy had fashioned an iron gate from a piece of an old picnic basket. Aaron was drawn in by this amazing work of art.

"Am I alive?" Aaron asked the boy.

He looked up at Aaron and smiled. "Only if you wish to be," the boy replied, and Aaron started down the sandy road leading to the front of the castle.

Before him, Aaron saw the thick wooden drawbridge, its

heavy chains arching gracefully up into the stone gatehouse wall. He started across ... but as he stopped to look over the edge, a feeling of unease chilled him: Far beneath him, like an opaque ribbon of glaucous jello, the forbidding moat wrapped the castle. Largely smothered by thick vegetation, the moat was undoubtedly home to an odious assortment of grotesque creatures – each doggedly waiting to administer a fabulously hideous death upon anyone unfortunate enough to take a plunge.

Aaron shuddered ... then he stepped back from the edge and walked on under the massive iron gate and into the castle gatehouse, where hidden pulleys and counterweights stood ready to help raise the drawbridge in the likely event of an attack.

Beyond the gatehouse Aaron entered the inner ward of the castle, which in this case was a vast inland ocean. The air was warm and soft. A sparkling ground-coral beach stretched a hundred yards in front of him and as far as he could see to his right and left. Puffy, cartoon clouds arched across the sky – like a great cotton canopy – forming the distant ceiling of the cavern.

The little black boy had followed him. Aaron turned and waved to him; the boy smiled and waved back.

Aaron walked slowly out to where the ocean waves were breaking and running up on the sand. The cool sea-water washed over his ankles and splashed up his legs.

He continued on, deeper and deeper into the water. It was fresh, invigorating and exceptionally clear. Soon his head was completely under – yet he had no trouble breathing. Rainbow schools of shimmering fish flew over the coral sculptures surrounding him.

A large, colorful grouper swam up to Aaron, its pectoral fins oscillating like a pair of silvery, Japanese hand fans.

Aaron looked at the fish curiously and asked, "Am I in Heaven?"

"Only if you wish to be," the grouper replied, its big, fish lips puckering as it spoke. Then it turned and slowly swam away.

Aaron smiled and continued on his wondrous journey.

He came upon a pirate ship with its Jolly Roger flying in the swift current flowing by the masthead. A badly decomposed, wooden CONDEMNED sign was nailed to the side of the ship above a gaping hole in the hull, where the ship, no doubt, was rammed during a desperate sea battle. Aaron stepped through into the darkness of the doomed ship's bowels.

Great stacks of supply barrels and coiled rope lined the inside of the vessel's hold, along with several swords, flintlock pistols, and automatic rifles. A store of green duffel bags filled a corner, stacks of $100 bills spilling from a split in one of them. A black plastic trash bag lay open, revealing its cache of treasure; Aaron reached in and found a leather wallet, but as he lifted it out it crumbled to dust.

Sprawled in every bearing, the skeletal remains of the unfortunate ship's crew. Inky eye-sockets followed Aaron as he moved through the sunken cemetery, their alabaster skulls grinning as if the scavengers feeding on their trailing flesh tickled.

Aaron noticed a plastic name tag stuck between the ribs of

one of the corpses. It read BANK MANAGER.

Hanging nearby (with no apparent means of support), Aaron found a rope macramé hammock, and suddenly he grew very tired. He climbed into it and fell deeply asleep.

Chapter 43

SALLY'S OR BUST

Ashley lay across the bed in Room 107, staring at the TV. The local station's weather man looked if he had been through the dry cleaners along with his suit. His forecast was for rain and high winds throughout the night.

NEWS FLASH:
A hostage was reported killed today during an armed robbery at the downtown branch of Community Plaza Bank. The murder took place at approximately 9:30 this morning. Witnesses said the gunmen wore the same brightly painted ski masks and carried assault rifles similar to the ones used in a series of robberies that took place in the city yesterday. Police have initiated a citywide manhunt.

Ashley took no notice of the report. She checked her watch. 6 p.m. She stood and turned off the TV, slipped the gun into her purse, grabbed her car keys, and stepped outside.

She paused on the sidewalk for a moment, scanning the parking lot as leaves and bits of trash bounced by on a wind gearing up for a heavy storm. Darkness was approaching and a light rain had begun to fall – and it was very cold. Ashley buttoned her light jacket, pulled up her collar, and turned to lock the door.

Suddenly a voice said, "Going somewhere?"

Ashley whirled around, expecting Death himself, but it was only the pint-sized proprietor of the Sands Motel: Doolin Mars, in his print pajamas.

"*Doolin!*" she cried, staggering back a step. "Damn you! Don't do that!"

She moved toward her Nova, favoring her ankle as she leaned into the wind, each step hurting. She could feel the loathsome creep following her.

"Can't talk now, Doolin," she said over her shoulder. "I'm in a hurry ..."

Doolin called after her into the wind. "I was hoping you'd have dinner with me tonight, Arlene."

My God, she thought, *this guy's unbelievable.* "Can't tonight ... I really have to go."

With a surprising burst of speed, Doolin ran around her and blocked her path. "I worked real hard preparing a special dinner for you," he said, breathless from the effort. "I expect you to show me the courtesy of –"

"Screw you, Doolin, you freaking weirdo. You're *insane!* Get out of my way."

Doolin stood firm, looking at Ashley with a puzzled expression on his face, as if surprised by her attitude.

Ashley shoved him aside. "I said *move,* you little fly!"

Doolin grabbed her arm with a grip that would leave a bruise, but Ashley twisted free. She fell back a step and pulled her gun, gripping it with both hands, aiming at Doolin's crotch.

"Keep your filthy paws off me, you slimy little bastard!" she screamed. *"Or I swear – I'll blow your fucking balls off!"*

Doolin stumbled backward, hands in the air. "Okay, okay," he said, "I get it. It's cool. I get it."

Ashley sighted on him as he moved away from her. "And *stay* away, you *maggot!* Leave me the *fuck* alone!"

She jumped in her Chevy, tossed the gun on the passenger seat, and started the engine. Then she slammed it in gear and floored it out of the parking lot – swearing never to return.

Chapter 44

RATHER DAPPER

Aaron jolted awake, terrified: One of the pirate skeletons had leaned over him and was shaking him by the shoulder with an osseous hand.

"*Aaron ...*" it hissed through gnashing teeth. "*Aaron, wake up ...*"

A cold, deep-ocean current moved through the ship like a limpid sea monster, rocking Aaron's hammock and sending a shiver through him. He cried out, delirious, clawing desperately at the hand on his shoulder.

"Aaron," the voice repeated, but sounding different. "Wake up. It's Willy. It's time to go."

Aaron gave a deep shuddering sigh and opened his eyes. Willy's familiar face emerged.

"Oh, *man* ..." Aaron said, looking around to get his bearings. "You wouldn't believe the weird dream I had." *More like the fantasies of a lunatic*, he thought.

Willy was torn between relief and anger; it hadn't been easy for him either. "It was *weird*, all right," he said. "I thought you were *OD-ing* or something. You were flying all over the couch, waffling on and on, and I couldn't understand a bloody thing you were saying. You really put the willies up me, mate."

He walked over to the sink and splashed some cold water

on his face, then returned with some damp paper towels and used them to cool Aaron's forehead.

"We need to go," he said. "The morphine should help for a few hours. Can you walk?"

Aaron pulled back the blanket and slowly sat up. "There's one way to find out," he said confidently. Then he carefully swung his feet out onto the floor.

He stood, pausing with his hand on the arm of the sofa, waiting for a wave of dizziness to pass. The table with the medical supplies was a few steps away, and he marked it as a goal. Then, with considerable effort, he shuffled to it and leaned on it for support as another wave of dizziness came and went.

His tongue was puffy and sticking to the roof of his mouth. "Can you get me some water?" he asked. "My mouth tastes like a handful of dried cat turds."

Willy laughed, happy to hear Aaron's humor returning. He poured him another glass. "Are you gonna be okay, mate?"

Aaron took several delicious sips of water, with short breaths between. Though still in considerable pain, and in spite of his dizziness, he was thinking clearly now, and he knew what had to be done. "I have to be," he replied.

Willy found a black wool overcoat draped over a chair and picked it up; it hung thick and heavy in his hands. He carried it over and showed it to Aaron.

"Look what I found," he said. "Try it on for size." He held the coat for Aaron as he slid an arm into one sleeve.

"It's warm," Aaron said, running a hand over the thick weave. The coat draped nearly to his ankles. "Thanks, Willy."

Willy rolled up the bulky sleeves for him and straightened the lapels. "I should say, old chap," he remarked. "You look rather dapper."

He shoved the bottle of morphine tablets into his pocket and picked up the lantern. "Are you ready?" he asked.

"Ready," Aaron replied bravely. "But there's some stuff we need to do on the way out."

"No problem," Willy said. "Lead the way."

Chapter 45

NOT A GOOD HIDEOUT

Aaron leaned on Willy as they made their way to the cannery's main-floor storeroom. Rain drummed the metal roof high overhead, and multiple streams of water poured through gaps in the sheeting and splashed on the floor below.

Aaron winced as a stab of pain cut through the morphine. "I'm sorry I was an asshole earlier," he said. "I don't know what happened to me."

Willy had to agree with him. "You really were being a shit, you know."

Aaron smiled and leaned on Willy a bit more.

The storeroom was full of loaded duffel bags. Aaron ran his hand over one of them and then sat down on it to rest.

"Check the other bags," he said. "We're looking for the one with guns in it."

"Guns?"

"We're not in Kansas anymore, Toto."

One by one, Willy opened the bags. The first contained white painter's jumpsuits, others miscellaneous gear.

He found a bag full of cash and held the lantern high above it, using his free hand to wipe his glasses on his shirt. "Check it out," he said, excited.

"Guns, Willy," Aaron said. "We're looking for guns."

Willy reluctantly closed the money bag and continued

searching.

He located the armory bag, reached in, and pulled out a shiny, black assault rifle. "Bloody hell, Aaron," he said, turning the weapon over in his hands. "You'd probably blow your damn willy off with one of these."

"Yeah – or yours," Aaron said. "Here, I'll take it ... the ammo should be in the same bag."

Willy handed him the gun then found a loaded magazine.

"Now, pay attention," Aaron said, and Willy watched in amazement as his friend demonstrated proper loading technique.

"... then insert the magazine into the slot below the trigger, here," Aaron continued, "and push it up from the bottom till it clicks. Give it a good smack to make sure it stays in, then yank on it to be sure." He showed Willy how to set the safety, then like a hardened soldier preparing for battle, slung the loaded rifle over his good shoulder.

"Okay ... now do yours," he said.

Willy pulled another rifle from the sack and did as he had been instructed. Aaron showed him how to hold the gun and release the safety.

"Okay, there's one more thing we need to do," Aaron said.

Willy held Aaron's arm over his shoulders, and they made their way outside to the boiler house.

"I remember this place," Willy said, adjusting the lantern's twin mantles for maximum light. "It's creepy in here. And it smells funny."

Aaron wrinkled his nose. "You're right, it does."

"Bring the light over here," Aaron said. "I helped Tom

repair one of these once."

Willy held the lantern high. "So, what are we doing?"

Aaron located the boiler's valve cluster. "We're going to blow this place to hell."

Willy thought about that for a moment and decided it made sense.

Aaron reached in and turned the pressure regulator adjustment knob all the way up. Then he disabled the pressure relief valve with a wrap of wire. The needle on the steam-pressure gauge started to rise.

"That should do it," he said. "Let's get the heck out of here."

Chapter 46

HIS WOMAN

Needles had taken the white van and gone to get burgers for himself and Beeks; he sat alone at a red light drinking a cup of coffee. His cell phone rang and he set the cup in a holder and answered the call.

"Needles," a woman's voice said, "this is Brandy."

Needles was quite surprised. "Well, hello, Brandy," he said politely.

"I'll get right to the point," she said. "You know about Johnny's meeting with that woman tonight, right?"

"At Sally's ... yes." He glanced at his watch. 6:02 p.m. "In just under half-an-hour."

"Well, I had lunch with him today, and he got drunk on his ass, and told me a lot more about that meeting than I wanted to hear."

"I'm listening," Needles said.

"You've heard how he and I first met, right?"

"At church, right? He was your Pastor."

"Well, that's not really how it happened."

Needles smiled. He wasn't surprised. The whole affair had been shadowy from the get-go, and he'd learned to take Souther's stories with a grain of salt.

"My real name is Barbara Fischer," Brandy explained. "Two weeks after my sixteenth birthday my parents and I had this huge fight, and I had seen this ad online for a modeling job at a new agency downtown and decided to check it out – you know, to get back at them."

Needles had no idea where this was going – and the smell of the food was making him hungry.

"So, anyway, the people were really nice, and they took a gazillion pictures of me. And, well, apparently they liked what they saw, because they sent me straight upstairs to the owner's office. And you won't believe who it was?"

The light turned green, and Needles plucked a few French fries from the bag and proceeded through the intersection.

"It was *Johnny Souther*," she said. "That's how we met."

Needles sat up in his seat.

"I was *totally* star struck," she went on, "and Mr. Souther knew he'd hooked me. So he came right out and told me that Black Eagle Studios was in reality a front for his prostitution ring, and that during my first shoot the photographer would be taking more than just pictures."

"You've got to be kidding me," Needles said.

"Yes ... and by then I couldn't back out, of course – I knew too much. Besides, I knew the money would be good, and I had *zero* desire to go back to my parent's house anyway. So he got me a place to stay and renamed me Brandy Fine, and I spent the next two days trying to psych myself up for my big debut."

Needles was speechless. *Johnny Souther, a pimp? How could I not have known about this?*

"... But then, at the last minute, Mr. Souther canceled everything and took me out for dinner and drinks – just the two of us – and we've been together ever since."

"So, what does this have to do with Ashley Quinn?"

Needles asked. But no sooner had he said it did it dawn on him.

"Can't you see?" Brandy said. "Johnny wouldn't go to all this trouble if all he wanted to do was *kill* Ashley."

"He'd have done that by now," Needles said. "And he's not thinking prostitution here ... he wants her all to himself."

"Right. And don't think for a moment that her son is out of the woods," Brandy said. "That *exchange* he promised her? It's *crap*. Johnny may be a sociopath, but he's not stupid. He knows he can make a lot of money with a pretty teenage boy."

Needles's stomach was in knots. "What about the digital recording? Why not just take her?"

Brandy gave a sad laugh. "Digital ... that's cute. He used to leave cassettes. Listen ... the recordings are one of Johnny's methods of courting a girl. For some weird reason he thinks they're clever – like that stupid hat. I think they're sick. I've heard him locked in his den recording them, and it makes we want to puke. He only makes tapes for the *special* girls – and they're the first to kick off when they reject him. I know this because I was friends with girls who got tapes right before they got iced. He wants to *have* her, Needles. And if she doesn't like it ... she's dead."

"But why the sudden compassion?" Needles asked, still struggling to digest it all. "Where were you when the other girls were in trouble?"

Compassion? Brandy thought. *Who said anything about compassion?*

"The others were never a real threat," she said proudly. "But Johnny has never lusted for *any* woman the way he lusts for Ashley Quinn – not even me. I saw her picture. I know she's gorgeous – probably smart, too. I don't need a woman like that strutting about in my territory. *I'm* his woman, okay? I've been his woman for ten years. And I will *be* his woman, until the day he fucking dies."

Needles grabbed another handful of fries and put the pedal down. He knew what he had to do.

Chapter 47

I CAN RIDE

Aaron and Willy dragged their bikes through the secret entrance to the outside, preparing for the ride across town to Sally's Diner.

Aaron stopped and took out his cell phone.

"What's up?" Willy asked.

"Do you remember Michael? The guy with the cool loft?"

Willy nodded.

"Yeah – well, he'd want to help us."

"You're right," Willy agreed. "He would."

Aaron gave him a puzzled look. Then he dug Michael's number out of his shoe, keyed in the number, and pressed CALL.

Michael was out roaming the city in desperate search of Aaron. His cell phone rang several times, but he couldn't answer it – his phone was back in his loft, in the pocket of his jacket where he had left it.

"He's not picking up," Aaron said sadly, pocketing his phone. They swung their loaded rifles around to their backs and climbed on the bikes.

Just then a pair of headlights swept around the far end of the cannery, temporarily blinding them. The boys froze like a pair of frightened deer, straddling their bikes, not knowing what to do.

It was Needles, alone behind the wheel of the white van.

He pulled up and skidded to a stop next to them.

He recognized Aaron and lowered his window. "What the hell are you —" He saw the rifles, and answered his own question. "Oh, you can't be serious ..."

He stepped out of the van, leaving the engine running. "Get in," he said. "We're going with you." He walked over to unlock the big roll-up door

The boys looked at each other, surprised.

"Did you say '*we*?'" Aaron asked.

"Beeks will want to come with us," Needles said.

Aaron inhaled rapidly as from a knife in the gut. "*Beeks is in there?*" he gasped, covering his wound with his hand.

"I think he's down in the practice range," Needles said. "You boys load up your bikes while I look for him. I'll just be a second."

He rolled the door up just enough to duck under it then disappeared into the cannery.

Willy's face had popped a sweat. "What should we do?" he whispered.

Aaron heard ominous groaning sounds coming from the direction of the boiler house. "Come on," he said, and they dropped their bikes and ran inside the warehouse after Needles.

He was lighting a lantern.

"Needles," Aaron said, coughing hard. "You don't understand. We gotta *leave!*"

"Listen," Needles said. "Beeks is the toughest son-of-a-bitch I've ever met. If there's a fight tonight, I want him there. You got that?" He checked his watch. "Souther said 6:30 ... it's 6:15. We have time. Wait here, and don't move till I get back."

He picked up the lantern and started toward the back of the

warehouse.

Aaron coughed hard again, but this time it really hurt. *"Needles!"* he cried desperately, clenching his teeth in pain. He gestured feebly in the direction of the boiler house.

"The boiler ... it's ..." He trailed off.

Needles stopped, turned and looked back, his face suddenly ashen, then said in a low, knowing voice, "What did you do ... ?"

Aaron stood with his arms limp at his sides, the weight of tears behind his eyes. How could he possibly admit what he'd done? How could he ever own up to something like that? It was supposed to have been a harmless prank. Nothing more. Just the death of an old building that was ready to die anyway.

"I-I rigged the boiler ..." he said at last. "It's going to explode."

"What?" Needles gasped, jerking his head in the direction of the boiler house. *"Have you lost your mind? Can't you undo it?"*

"It's too late, Needles. I can hear –"

"Damn it!" Needles said, his attention returning to Beeks. "You two go on without me." He set the lantern on the floor and took off running, disappearing into the darkness of the cannery.

Aaron was numb. He stared at the empty space that had been Needles.

Willy heard the boiler. He put his hand on Aaron's shoulder. "You know we can't go after him, Aaron ..."

"I know."

"We gotta jet ..."

"I know."

"Can you ride?"

Aaron just stood there staring after Needles, the light from the lantern showing on his face. His fatigue was intense. He hadn't really slept in three days ... and now this. He had nothing left. He was ready to lie down right there on the cannery floor and die.

Willy took him gently by the shoulders and looked him in the eye. "Aaron, listen to me. Your mother needs us, okay? *Can you ride?*"

Aaron looked at him oddly for a long moment; then his eyes sharpened and he slowly gathered himself and answered the question.

"I can ride."

Chapter 48

HIGH PRESSURE

Needles arrived at the practice range out of breath. The hatch was open, and that light was shining up from down below.

He called down the steps. "Beeks!"

Beeks couldn't hear a thing under his earmuffs.

POP! POP! POP! Three rounds through the bulls-eye.

"*Beeks!*" Needles shouted.

No response.

"*Damn it!*"

He started down the ladder, then stopped short when he heard a loud metallic, groaning sound. Then a tremendous *bang* made him shiver, and he climbed quickly down the ladder.

POP! POP! Two more rounds through the bull's-eye.

Needles ran over and yanked the earmuffs off Beeks's head.

Beeks nearly shot him in the face. "What the *fuck?*" he said.

"We have to get the hell out of here, Beeks!" Needles said. "The boiler's about to explode!"

"*What?*"

"Come on!"

Beeks mumbled something under his breath then dropped everything and followed Needles up the ladder. Needles climbed up out of the hatch then turned back to assist Beeks.

Beeks missed a step and banged his shin hard. *"Motherfucker!"* he exclaimed, biting his lower lip in pain.

"Come on, Beeks! Move your fat ass!"

The groaning sounds became an intense rumble that moved through the earth beneath them like a demon locomotive on a trip through hell. Needles held out his hand to help his oversized friend, then went cold when he heard a long, metallic, ear-grinding scrape, like a ship running aground on a rocky point. He looked over his shoulder toward the boiler house, then back down the hatch at Beeks. Beeks could see their fate reflected in his eyes.

Another low, shuddering rumble shook the building ... then *BOOM!*

The force of the blast smashed through the cannery like a great wrecking ball. Splintered brick and shards of steel shot through the structure like the shrapnel from a thousand mortar shells, ripping Needles to pieces as he was flailed to the floor. Beeks flew backward down the ladder and hit the ground on his neck, snapping his spine. The massive, steel boiler tank rocketed into the desiccated water tower, which then smashed its full weight through the cannery's sheet-metal roof, causing a chain-reaction collapse of the floors and interior walls. Burning embers ignited by the furnace sprayed out over the wood-framed structure, starting ancillary fires fed by shattered lanterns and sheared-off natural-gas lines. A tornado-like firestorm, hot enough to melt iron, burned the Alton Brothers Fish Cannery, along with the two trapped men, to a smoldering shell.

Chapter 49

DISTANT THUNDER

The rains had come again, and by the time Aaron and Willy reached the downtown area, they were pedaling through a downpour.

As they rode past the Community Plaza Bank building, Aaron checked the big clock. 6:25 p.m. They had to hurry.

Suddenly, from the distant waterfront, a huge flash, like a great nuclear flashbulb, lit up the surrounding buildings. There was a powerful, yet muffled boom – like that of distant thunder – but the boys knew that this was no thunderstorm. They skidded to a stop in the middle of the street, looked back and watched, horrified, as an irregular pattern of smaller flashes followed the first ... then the corresponding booms ... the ground beneath their feet shuddering with each concussion.

Finally the explosions subsided, and though there was much to say, the frightened boys were unable to utter even a single word.

They rode on, their ghostly shadows, cast by the hellish-red glow of the sky behind them, leading the way.

In the distance, sirens ..;

Chapter 50

THE DINER

The green canvas awning hanging over Sally's Diner flapped violently in the wind like a grossly overweight bird attempting to take flight. The neon OPEN sign, protected from the heavy rain by the diner's plate-glass front window, blinked a sad welcome.

Inside, out of the weather, occupying his usual spot at the counter, was Michael St. John. One of only two customers that night, he had stopped off at Sally's on the way home after scouring the city in search of Aaron.

To Michael's left, an angular old man in a gray wool suit read a coffee-stained copy of yesterday's *Times* through tired eyes enlarged by thick lenses. Long white hair flew wildly about his head, suggestive of Albert Einstein. A glazed donut on a saucer before him bled cherry jelly.

Michael's swivel perch afforded him a panoramic view of the kitchen.

The cook, his face shiny and swollen from the heat of the grill, concentrated on the job at hand. Beads of sweat balanced on his bald head as he worked his spatula, flipping burgers in a shimmering pool of grease that splattered the front of his distended T-shirt with every turn. Bits of decaying lettuce clung to his shoes as he walked over and gave the empty order wheel a spin. He refilled Michael's coffee then returned to the grill as several roaches scurried to safety.

With one hand Michael held a novel; with the other he

pulled sugar packets from a ceramic bowl and stacked them into a precarious tower.

If only I'd called the police that first night, he thought, *maybe I could have helped him.* But in his heart he knew it may have made things worse.

He added another sugar packet to his tower then returned to the top of the same page he had reread several times before.

Ashley's rumpled Nova slowed and parked out front behind Michael's Aston.

She checked her watch. 6:25 p.m.

Through the downpour the diner door was a ghostly apparition. It called to her – as if it wished to devour her.

She drew in a tight breath of air, then picked up the gun lying on the passenger seat, pausing to consider her options. But she was incapable of putting a rational thought together, so she placed the gun in the glove box and stepped out into the rain.

The diner's front door swung open, ringing a small bell and rattling the blinds. Michael's sugar tower fell.

He turned and saw a slender, attractive young woman walk through the door. She removed her damp, faux-suede jacket to reveal a simple, short sundress, hemmed a hand's width above the knee, that hung lightly over the curves of her breasts and hips. Inexpensive and a bit inappropriate for the current weather, he observed, but clean and *very* flattering. She wore simple eyeglasses that made her large eyes even larger. Michael's beloved wife, Jennie, had worn glasses, and he had always thought they added an innocence that he found enchanting.

Visibly anxious, the woman smoothed her dress with hands both delicate and strong. She removed her glasses, and as she leaned down to dry them using the hem of her dress, Michael couldn't help noticing the little price tag hanging from the zipper down her back. She wore a simple wedding band, but on her right hand.

She was obviously in some kind of trouble: her mascara was smudged, the area below her right eye bruised. Still, Michael could see the clear light of intelligence in her eyes, and found himself completely enamored of her.

Ashley pulled strands of damp brown hair back from her face and looked cautiously around the room.

The diner was dimly lit, cramped, and hot – the air hanging heavily over the mismatched booths and tables like the breath of an old troll.

To her left, a rabbit-eared TV struggled to maintain a failing image amid dusty, burned out beer signs. To the right, on the far side of the large front window, hung a full-wall mosaic of the American flag, its red, white, and blue tiles surprisingly intact considering the condition of the rest of the diner. Cut into the mural below the field of stars was a door upon which the unisex restroom symbol had been crudely painted in white enamel.

Toward the back, separating the dining area from the smoke-filled kitchen, was a long, Formica counter with aluminum edging and a row of stools – each with its pitted-chrome base bolted securely to the floor, the cracked red-vinyl seats mended with rough duct-tape patches.

Her heart stopped when for a moment she thought she saw Johnny Souther sitting at the counter. She looked again and was relieved to see that it was just a handsome stranger.

She limped over and took a seat a couple of stools to Michael's right. She set her purse on the counter and laid her jacket next to it.

Michael tried his best to be discreet, but he couldn't take his eyes off of her, and when she repositioned herself – irritated, no doubt, by the cracked vinyl against the soft, smooth skin of her thighs – he felt weak.

Ashley checked her watch again. 6:28 p.m. She glanced at Michael then looked away so he wouldn't see the despair on her face.

He leaned in her direction and spoke in a low, comfortable voice. "You know ... you're putting your life at risk eating here."

"Is that so?" Ashley said, pausing to check the front door.

"If I were you, I'd run like hell." He laughed to himself and started a new sugar stack. "I haven't seen you in here before. Do you live nearby?"

"No," she said, clearly distracted.

"I eat here all the time," Michael said then thought of how that must have sounded. "Not that I'm proud of it or anything."

"Good for you." Ashley said, wishing this guy would just leave her alone.

Michael swiveled back toward the kitchen, his attempts at humor clearly under appreciated.

"Hey, chef!" he said. "My dinner?"

The cook flipped him off, but Michael only smiled. Over the years he had formed a quasi-friendship with the cook and he'd grown accustomed to his stiff-finger-salute.

He decided to give the woman another go. He marked his page and slid over to the stool next to her.

"I'm Michael," he said, offering his hand. "Michael St. John." At close range she smelled wonderful.

Ashley looked down without shaking his hand and folded hers in her lap. "I'd rather be alone, thank you."

Michael stood and raised his hands slightly. He was disappointed, but remained cool. "I've got no problem with that," he said pleasantly.

He sensed that the woman had been quite fun and playful when she was younger but had no doubt suffered terrible misfortunes over the years, and he could see a deep sadness in her eyes. But he knew that the playful girl must still be hiding inside her somewhere, and to him that made her even more captivating. He smiled politely then returned to his original stool, where he picked up his paperback and flipped to his mark.

Ashley's eye's moistened – she hadn't intended to take her frustrations out on him. "I'm sorry," she said, dabbing her nose with a tissue. "You seem like a nice enough guy, and under normal circumstances I'd be flattered."

She paused ... it had been a long time since she talked to a man in that way – and it felt good. Then, on a wild impulse, she shared a piece of her dangerous secret with him.

"The truth is," she said, "I came down here to this rat-hole to save my son."

Michael dropped his book and looked at her. "Hold on a second," he said, then paused – this would be too wild a coincidence. "You're not Ashley Quinn by any chance – are you? You're not *Aaron's* mom ..."

Oh my God, Ashley thought, her hand to her throat. She stood, her face filled with astonishment. "How did you ... I mean –"

"It's okay," Michael said quickly, sensing her panic. "I met Aaron the other night. We're friends. I've been looking for him, too."

Ashley was dumbfounded, then frightened as she remembered Johnny Souther's orders and shot a glance at the door. "I-I can't be seen talking to you," she said, stepping away from the counter. Then she grabbed her purse and ran to the restroom.

Just then the cook delivered Michael's burger. "Choke on it ..." he said, anticipating a retort.

But Michael only looked at him, dazed.

Chapter 51

THE SHOWDOWN

Michael jumped when suddenly the diner's front door banged open again. The little brass bell flew off its hook and bounced across the room, coming to rest near his feet.

Johnny Souther entered and casually removed his sodden overcoat. Rainwater dripped from the brim of his leather fedora, staining his jacket; he removed the hat and tossed it on a table, then draped the overcoat over the back of a chair.

He glanced at Michael – who averted his eyes – then he knocked some dirty dishes and trash off onto the floor, and sat down alone.

He checked his watch. 6:30 p.m. His hip was hurting again and he badly needed a cup of coffee. He pounded the table with a heavy fist.

"Doesn't anybody work in this dump?" he said.

The cook glared at him through a burger haze. "Hey, you ... Put a lid on it."

Souther hadn't taken time out of his busy day to come to the diner and fight with some cook; but once provoked, it was impossible for him to back down.

"I'm sorry," he said coolly, rising slowly to his feet. "I must be hard of hearing." He tilted his head slightly and cupped his hand behind his ear in a subtle show of aggression. "Could you repeat that?"

The cook approached the counter and leaned on his broad, course hands, nearly upsetting Michael's coffee cup. He looked directly into Souther's eyes and calmly rephrased his statement.

"I said, 'put a lid on it' ... *asshole*."

Off his stool, now, Michael backed toward the restroom. The old man with the jelly donut folded his paper.

Souther casually pulled his .45 automatic and pointed it at the cook.

The cook seized a heavy, cast-iron skillet from the stove and hurled it at his assailant before ducking behind the counter. Like a huge cast-iron Frisbee, the pan impacted the far wall of the diner with a violent clang, sending the TV and several beer signs crashing to the floor.

Two shots shattered the air – the first striking the order wheel, sending it spinning, the other ricocheting off the stainless-steel panel behind the grill. The old man laid his head on the counter and wrapped it in his arms.

A third shot rattled some kitchen utensils, and Michael made for the restroom.

He slammed the restroom door behind him and locked it, then crouched, breathless, next to the single gray toilet stall. A pair of women's shoes showed beneath the panel. They were shaking.

Michael leaned back against the wall and swallowed hard, trying to think, but his mind was like a Scrabble board that'd been knocked to the floor. A fat spider scurried across the grimy gray paint next to his ear.

A heavy thud echoed from the diner. Michael crept forward and peeked through a crack in the doorjamb.

Souther had thrown a table up on its side. The cook stood and heaved another pan, then sprinted for the back door. The pan bounced harmlessly off Souther's shield and he stood and fired.

The cook's head exploded like a melon thrown from a speeding train as bits of brain and bone sprayed the kitchen walls. The old man with the donut fainted and slumped to the floor.

Souther walked calmly toward the kitchen and emptied his .45 into the cook and tossed the gun on the counter. Then he leaned in and yanked a meat cleaver from a block and turned toward the restroom, the razor-sharp blade glistening as it hung from the end of his powerful arm.

Michael scanned the tiny restroom for an exit. He saw a window above the sink, but he judged it to be too narrow.

Suddenly the door shook as someone tried the knob.

Michael froze.

Then, with enormous strength, the intruder attacked the door. Splinters flew as a heavy blade penetrated the wood.

Michael's mind worked frantically. He saw a urinal, a sink, a mirror with no glass, the window, and the single toilet stall containing the terrified woman.

"Unlock the stall door," he said to her. "*Quickly!*"

The bolt slid back, and with a heave, Michael hoisted the heavy steel gate from its pins and stepped back behind the restroom door. Utterly exposed, Ashley cowered in the narrow space next to the toilet, her thin, pale arms covering her head.

With a brutal crash, Johnny Souther burst through the door – eyes bloody with rage.

Ashley screamed and Michael wielded his weapon.

The sharp corner of the stall door caught Souther's skull just above the ear, sending the cleaver clattering across the tile. He expelled a sickening groan and crumpled heavily into a heap.

Michael staggered back against the wall, his heart trying to beat its way out of his chest. Ashley stared wide-eyed at the pool of blood spreading over the tiles beneath Souther's head. She leaned over and vomited into the toilet.

Michael stepped through the mangled restroom door into a quiet diner. Streaks of blood drained down the panel behind the stove and mixed with the grease on the grill, creating swirling patterns. The contorted image of the old man was mirrored in the chrome at the base of the stool where he lay. Michael took a seat on his favorite stool.

Ashley stood in the restroom doorway looking at him, wiping her mouth with one hand, adjusting her rumpled sundress with the other. He swiveled in her direction and their eyes met.

Suddenly, from behind her, Johnny Souther appeared, his face obscured by blood. He held the meat cleaver high overhead, ready to bury it in the back of Ashley's skull.

"*BEHIND YOU!*" Michael cried, jumping to his feet.

Ashley turned and screamed.

From outside, twin blasts of automatic-rifle fire shattered the front plate-glass window and sent Souther careening into the counter. Ashley spun away in horror as blood spattered her face and clothing.

Souther opened his mouth to scream, but no sound came as he twisted in agony, clawing the bloody countertop with his fingernails before dropping to the floor with a sickening flump, where he lay still ... in a lifeless sprawl.

Chapter 52

A RAGGED SAVAGE

Michael and Ashley stared in shock and loathing at Souther's mutilated body ... the floor ... the walls ... themselves. At last they turned toward the front of the diner.

Framed in the opening where the large window had been were two young boys. Thin gray wisps of smoke curled from the over-heated barrels of the assault rifles they held in their hands. Behind them, on the sidewalk in the rain, lay an old BMX bike and a rusty beach cruiser – spoked wheels still spinning.

The taller of the two boys looked hardly more than a ragged savage – his eyes dark, his face gaunt, his hair matted. A coal black, rain-soaked overcoat hung on him like a heavy blanket thrown over a tombstone. The front of the coat draped open, revealing a crimson rose that bloomed in the center of the large white bandage wrapping his chest.

Ashley was stunned. Tears welled in her eyes and her hand moved to her mouth. "*Aaron?*" she said, but he was oblivious.

She stepped through the window and went to her son.

"Aaron?" she said, softly. "Aaron, honey – it's me ... it's Mommy." She carefully removed the rifle from his hands and laid it on the sidewalk. Then she took him gently in her arms and held him.

"I'm sorry," Aaron said at last, his voice soft and hoarse.

"Shhh," she said, her eyes flooding with tears. "No apologies, okay? I love my little boy. I love him with all my heart."

Aaron buried himself in his mother's warmth and cried the deeply mournful cry of a long lost boy come home.

Willy stood alone, staring unblinking at Souther's broken body through smudged glasses. The diner's neon OPEN sign lay in pieces among the shards of glass at his feet.

Michael went over and knelt next to him on the sidewalk. He took the rifle and set it carefully aside, and then he rested his hand on the boy's shoulder and spoke softly to him. "Willy – it's Michael ... It's over ... you're safe, now."

Willy was struck mute.

Michael tried to appear lighthearted. "I think we better get the heck out of here before the cops come," he said. "Is that all right with you, Willy?"

Willy looked up at Michael and nodded.

"Stay right here and don't move," Michael said. "I'll be right back."

Michael collected the two rifles and stepped into the diner.

Aaron followed him inside.

Michael laid the firearms on the counter, then reached in and used a towel to pick up a pan full of hot oil, which he poured over the guns, coating them completely.

Aaron walked over to Souther's grisly corpse and knelt next to it. Then he calmly went through the pockets until he found what he was looking for: the precious photo of his mother and father together in the alpine meadow.

Chapter 53

ANYWHERE

The rain had stopped, and the night air was calm and crisp. A brilliant moon ducked in and out of patchy gray clouds, highlighting the edges a snowy white.

Michael and Aaron exited Sally's Diner through the front door and joined Willy and Ashley on the sidewalk. Ashley had been talking with Willy and he was feeling much better.

Michael handed Ashley her jacket and purse, and a clean towel.

She clutched them to her chest and smiled at him, forming two little dimples in her cheeks that he hadn't seen before. "Thank you," she said, truly grateful. She turned away briefly and used the towel to wipe her face and clean her glasses.

When she turned back, Michael surprised her by gently brushing the hair back from her face with the backs of his fingertips. She hesitated – but she didn't resist. She hadn't really thought of him in that way before, but it felt natural and she liked it.

Michael helped her with her jacket then gazed deeply into her large eyes with a look that said, *I can only imagine what you've been through, Ashley ... and I'm very sorry*. She returned his gaze and smiled to herself, a soothing warmth swelling in her heart.

He took her hand, and then, delicately, in a voice as gentle as a kiss, he said, "Could I drive you somewhere?"

Her eyes remained locked on his, but her head turned ever

so slightly downward and to the side. "Thank you, Michael," she replied, moistening her perfect lips and drawing them back into a provocative smile. "Anywhere ..."

Chapter 54

NOT THE CATS AGAIN

"Shouldn't we be leaving or something?" Willy said, checking the street.

Michael started then remembered where he was. He held Ashley's hand a moment longer, smiling at her. "You're right, Willy," he said. "We should go."

He glanced at the two bikes on the sidewalk, then at his sports car. "Sorry guys," he said. "We'll have to leave the bikes."

Aaron and Willy looked at each other and frowned.

"But as soon as we get a chance ..." he said, pausing for effect, "... we're going shopping for new ones."

"Awesome!" the boys said together, exchanging a delighted look, their frowns flipped to grins.

Aaron turned and gave Willy a hug.

"What was that for?" Willy said, cocking his head.

"Oh, nothing ... I just felt it," Aaron replied. "Oh, and whenever you're ready to go get a burger, you let me know."

Willy grinned from ear to ear. His best friend was back.

Ashley put both arms around the boys and kissed them on the tops of their heads. "I'll be back in a second," she said.

She retrieved the gun from the Nova's glove box then kicked it under the curb and down the storm drain. Then she hopped back over with the others.

Michael touched the OPEN zone on his wristwatch and the DBS sizzled to life with an impressive show of British technology.

Willy grinned bigger than he had in years. He was proud of his homeland and wished he could hop in and drive the impressive machine. But, for him, just standing next to this incredible work of art was an experience to be cherished. "I *love* this car," he said, practically drooling down the door.

Michael helped Aaron slide into the shotgun seat, while Ashley and Willy happily squeezed into the back from the driver's side.

Aaron looked south, toward the waterfront. The distant horizon still glowed as the fires consuming the Alton Brothers Fish Cannery burned themselves out. He shuddered when for a moment the horrors of the last three days swept over him like the cold shadow of Death.

He thought of Needles and Beeks and smiled sadly. They had saved his life. And in their own unique ways, they, together with Willy, had unearthed in him an inner strength he might never have discovered on his own.

He turned and looked at his mother, then at Michael, and a deep feeling of contentment settled over him, contentment he hadn't known for many years. Who could have imagined that three horrific days would become a miraculous new beginning.

Michael settled in behind the wheel and closed the door with a solid whump. He inserted the sapphire-crystal key and pressed the starter button.

"Hey, Mom ..." Aaron said, over his shoulder. "Did Michael tell you about the old lady he saw pushing a wheelbarrow full of cats down the street?"

"No ... I don't think so," she replied, amused by the question.

"Sounds like a good premise for your first novel," Michael said.

Aaron smiled at him thoughtfully then said to himself: *And so it shall be!*

"Anyway," he continued, "they were all different colored house cats, and it was raining and they were all wet, and, and –"

"What a load of crap," Willy said.

"– and there was this one cat, and he was the biggest cat in the whole world ..."

Michael hit the throttle and everyone laughed along with Aaron as together they sped off into the night.

In the distance, sirens ...

THREE DAYS TO DIE

John Avery

About the Author

John Avery lives with his wife, Julie, on a small ranch in the mountains outside San Diego with their horses, dogs, and chickens.

John thanks you for reading Three Days to Die and sincerely hopes you enjoyed it.

www.ingramcontent.com/pod-product-compliance
Lightning Source LLC
Chambersburg PA
CBHW050929120626
46552CB00001B/108

9 7 8 0 9 8 3 6 9 6 3 0 8